By JON KEYS

Home Grown
Heart of the Pines
Obsidian Sun

Published by DREAMSPINNER PRESS
http://www.dreamspinnerpress.com

OBSIDIAN SUN

JON KEYS

Published by
DREAMSPINNER PRESS

5032 Capital Circle SW, Suite 2, PMB# 279, Tallahassee, FL 32305-7886 USA
http://www.dreamspinnerpress.com/

This is a work of fiction. Names, characters, places, and incidents either are the product of author imagination or are used fictitiously, and any resemblance to actual persons, living or dead, business establishments, events, or locales is entirely coincidental.

Obsidian Sun
© 2015 Jon Keys.

Cover Art
© 2015 Paul Richmond.
http://www.paulrichmondstudio.com
Cover content is for illustrative purposes only and any person depicted on the cover is a model.

ISBN: 978-1-63476-291-5
Digital ISBN: 978-1-63476-292-2
Library of Congress Control Number: 2015905849
First Edition July 2015

Printed in the United States of America
∞
This paper meets the requirements of
ANSI/NISO Z39.48-1992 (Permanence of Paper).

GLOSSARY

TALAC TERMS

Akhir—Offensive magic from a Spellspinner against an attacker. It strips all emotion from the person and kills them. The backlash against the spinner is fatal, other than a few individuals through history.

Arrowweavers—Talac who specialize in creating the tribal longbows and arrows.

Blessed ones—The deities of the Talac.

Bloodfruit—Deep red berries found on the grasslands. They're considered a treat.

Bloodweaving—Ritual revenge. The pair declaring a bloodweaving must petition the gods for their blessing. The pair declaring the bloodweaving are bound to it until they fulfill the quest, or die trying.

Cloudflyers—Colorful flying insects that move in large swarms.

Corcra—The emotions of intimacy. It presents itself in the spinning as shades of purple.

Crawlers—Tiny biting pests that could infest the bedding and velvet of the Talac if the proper spells are not performed.

Daggerhorns—Grazing animals of the Talac homelands. Medium sized and brown in coloration, the animals are known for their long horns that are tipped with poison.

Deathspinner—Large spiders similar in size to two adult fists. They live in large colonies and create landscapes of webbing to trap their prey. Their silk can be harvested and is a critical element in the Talac magic.

Featherleaf trees—A low growing tree commonly found along permanent waterways in the Talac savanna. They are a deciduous tree with bipinnate leaves.

Featherweeds—Perennial plants with large, waist high leaves with deep separations.

First Spinner—One half of the Talac avatars to the gods.

First Twining—The combination of First Spinner and First Weaver.

First Weaver—One of the pair of avatars of the Blessed Ones of the Talac.

Great Weaving—The Talac afterlife, where a person's life fibers go before being woven into a new life.

Guardian bush—Head high bushes thickly covered by toxic barbed thorns. The toxin paralyzes chest muscles and stops the victims' breathing.

Herdweavers—Young Talac of both sexes who watch over the herds of kuri. They are armed with slings as their primary weapon against predators.

Hollow fruit—A melon native to the savanna with a hollow center filled with seeds.

Hunter grass—A coarse perennial grass used by the Kuri to make baskets.

Iceweaver—The deity of winter and the season of telling oral traditions. Also used as the common term for the cold season.

Ironwood tree—A medium sized tree with palm sized leaves and a very dense cell structure in its wood. The tree also absorbs silica from the soil and deposits it in the tissue.

Kit—The term used for Talac children who haven't reached puberty.

Kuri—The grazing herd animals raised by the Kuri class of the Talac people. Kuri is also the name of the clan who specialize in rearing the animals.

Longtooth—Predatory mammals that hunt in packs. They are tan in color with long tails used as counterbalance as they run. They have retractable claws and long incisor teeth that extend far past their bottom jaw.

Matama—Emotions given off by people. These are gathered by Spellspinners and combined with deathspinner silk for the spell weavings created by the Spellweavers.

Mezi—Same sex pairing. The terms are specific to the pairing, not the person. So a person who is bisexual could be either mezi or nisa, depending on the gender of their pairing. There is no stigma or significance for either among the Talac.

Nisa—Opposite sex pairing.

Pairing-bond—An almost telepathic connection between twined mates. In some cases they can share the harvested emotions via their connection.

Rattleback—A medium sized mammal that has their offspring four at a time. The name comes from the finger-thick spikes that cover the animal's back and make noise when they hit each other.

Rugza—The harvested threads of anger or violence. Usually not harvested other than in times of dire need.

Spellspinners—Talac who are born without the hallmark velvet of the other Talac. They are trained from birth to spin the fibers of emotions that are made by other people. But they can only spin the fibers; they cannot create weavings of magic.

Spellweavers—Talac who have the special sight needed to create spells from fibers spun by the spellspinners. Spellweavers discover they have the ability at puberty and are trained. They also are the type of Talac who are covered on almost all of their body with plush hair finer than velvet. At puberty they also get their adult velvet, which is a rich pattern of spirals and marks unique to each spellweaver.

Springtail—A small mammal common throughout the region. They have a distinctive upright carriage and muscular hindlegs that can allow them to jump many times their own height. They are a common quarry for young Talac who are learning to hunt.

Staffweaver—Talac who were trained to fight with a bladed staff. The tradition has been lost to the Kuri clan for several generations.

Strands—Mild profanity.

Sunbird—Smaller, bright yellow bird that move in flocks of several hundred.

Talac—A group of seminomadic people who form a number of clans based on a weaving specialization. Most of the Talac are born with a very short covering of hair, referred to as velvet, that forms detailed swirling patterns covering their body. A minority of the Talac are born with no velvet, which marks them as a spellspinner. The other half of the Talac magic is formed by spellweavers, who are identified when they reach puberty.

Twined Ones—The reference to First Weaver and First Spinner as a collective.

Twining (societal)—The rituals typically performed by a couple to formally announce their bond to each other. It also creates a physical connection between the couple. The strength of the connection varies from couple to couple.

Twining (weaving)—A weaving technique where two or more flexible elements cross over each other as they cross the warp threads, or spokes in basketry.

Unraveling—Ritual for sending the dead to the afterlife.

Warp—The elements of a weaving that are generally under tension and provide the structure for the weaving.

Weft—The thread that traverses the warp threads in order to create cloth.

VARAS TERMS

Burning Twins—Primary gods of the Varas. Also called the Red Twins or Red Gods.

Forever Words—The written sacred teachings of the Red Twins.

High Regency—Highest rank of the Varas ruling class. Somewhat of a figurehead as most of the power in the Varas culture rests with the slavers who can provide Talac slaves.

House of the Sun—The highest caste of the Varas. The High Regency is always from this caste.

Red Gods—Another term used for the gods worshiped by the Varas.

Red Twins—Primary gods of the Varas. Also called the Burning Twins or Red Gods.

River Serpent—Large aquatic animal. Adults are longer than two people tall. The Varas believe it is the Red God personified and sacrifice people to it by throwing them in the river.

Sun-drenched Talac—A Talac whose velvet is a golden blond rather than the typical brown. It's a rare occurrence and highly valued by the Varas.

Varas—A people with extensive permanent towns flanking the Great River. Many of the Varas are addicted to sex with the Talac who have velvet. As a result they have an extensive slave culture to meet the demand for sex slaves or houses of pleasure.

CHAPTER ONE

ANAN EASED into bow range. He'd been hunting for a fingercount of days and stalking this daggerhorn since the early gray of predawn. He waited until the animal turned away before rising to a crouch. The lethally armed grazer would feed him and his mate for days. He brought his bow up slowly and drew the bowstring to his cheek.

His body convulsed with pain that felt as if he'd been stabbed with a red-hot iron blade, and his arrow shot several lengths above his quarry, which disappeared into the deep grass.

In the next instant, Anan knew. His mating-bond with Silbre had snapped. Agony filled him, sending him to his knees as the bow slipped from his numb hands. Gasping for air, he dropped forward onto his hands as waves of loss and pain overwhelmed him.

I have to find Silbre. What happened? Our mating-bond can't be broken. Unwilling to believe the horrible truth, Anan had to find his mate.

He staggered to his feet, looping the bow over his shoulder as he took the first stumbling steps toward home. The surety of his pace came back to him, and he gained speed until he was sprinting toward the clan's encampment. Time became irrelevant. He walked when his legs refused to run and ate when his body demanded it.

Dusk came on him stealthily, but he refused to stop. *Silbre can't be gone. We've been together since our adult velvet.* Anan's chest tightened at the thought of losing his mate. His mind swirled with fear, horror, and anger. If their teachers hadn't sent him on yet another hunting trip, maybe he could have saved Silbre. No, he refused to believe he'd lost Silbre. There must be another explanation. He pushed down the rush of emotions and focused on

1

the run as night deepened. With the rise of the moons, he picked up speed, desperate to reach home.

Anan neared the last of his endurance when he saw the familiar featherleaf trees that lined the river bend where the Kuri clan spent its summers. He topped the river embankment and dropped to his knees at the sight before him. Complete devastation. The warm morning breeze carried the scent of death. The raucous voices of carrion birds as they fought over bits of his clan reinforced his horror.

He struggled down the steep embankment to splash through the shallow river that circled most of what had been the Kuri's summer encampment. As he waded to shore, he found the eyeless face of a childhood friend. Anan stumbled to one side and emptied his stomach. He retched again and again as he surpassed the limit of his emotional endurance until each twist of his stomach yielded nothing.

Silbre! Where's Silbre? Anan renewed his headlong flight to find his twining mate.

He ran through the devastation, sending flocks of birds into the air. With each heartbeat his desperation grew as he ran to their tent. *He has to be alive. I can't survive without him.* He rounded a pile of debris and found the familiar woven pattern of their summer lodge. His world died. Entangled in the remains, Silbre's body bristled with a fingercount of crossbow quarrels. *Varas slavers. Those are their bolts.* The iron heads and spiral fletching left no doubt. But they had never come this far into Talac territory.

Anan dropped to his knees and pulled Silbre tight against him. Anan's breath rasped between clenched teeth, his chest tight with grief as he rocked with his mate in his arms. A freshet of tears rolled over the plush hair covering his face. The dull drone from hordes of green burrowing flies and the cries of carrion birds surrounded him. But grief paralyzed Anan.

His sorrow merged with anger, and he screamed toward the implacable sky. "Why have you let this happen? Why did you cut his threads so short?"

Anan dropped his chin against his chest and sobbed. He rocked his mate slowly, tracing the tips of his fingers along the swirls of a spellweaver created in the short tan and brown hair covering Silbre's face while he fought to ignore the fatal wounds. Anan's throat tightened as more tears rolled down his cheeks. He lowered Silbre gently, as if he were sleeping.

The aftermath of the attack must be dealt with. He had no choice. He steeled himself to the carnage around him and struggled to understand. *How did the Varas unravel the protective web that surrounded the village? Especially those of the Kuri clan, who have some of the most skilled spellweavers of the Talac people.* Even if they had broken the spell, a warning would have been felt, and people would have boiled out like stingers from their nest. Something in the web of Anan's reality shifted as he wondered how the Varas were able to decimate a Talac village.

Anan called on his spell vision and tried to trace any threads, but they were gone. If there were survivors, they were no longer connected to the village weaving. He began moving in a haze of disbelief.

All the people he'd grown up with were gone. Saritua who taught him his first weavings, Trebea who knew the perfect day to harvest wood for bows that wouldn't wrack in the fall rains—gone. He'd never hear Poza talking with her imaginary friends as she toddled from one rug to another pretending at grownup, or her wonder when the spring gliders migrated across the savanna.

He'd seen the carrion birds pecking the flesh from their lifeless bodies. The horrors no longer registered, as his surroundings became part of an unending cascade of atrocities. At some point he would break and mourn. But not now; he was too numb, too overwhelmed. The bits of his being that weren't focused on what he had to accomplish in this moment hid in the corner of his mind, gibbering in near madness. Silbre couldn't come to the rescue this time. The task fell on his shoulders. There was no one else.

Screaming birds took off and revealed the burned arms of a spellspinner. With this final revelation, the last warp threads of Anan's reality snapped. All the Kuri spinners would be dead. When spellspinners in battle ripped the matama from the attackers, they condemned themselves to death. Akhir gave their attackers a painful end, but the backlash left the spellspinners burned and dead. He moved closer and saw the velvetless skin that marked them from birth as spellspinners. But the curse, or gift, of akhir created the final separation between the Talac spinners and weavers.

Anan's questionable skill at spellweaving didn't matter any longer. Without a spinner, there was no one to take the deathspinner eggs and harvest silk for the matama threads he needed for his weavings. Only the spinners knew how to combine matama with silk harvested from the most feared animals of the savanna. Without spun threads, Anan's years of training didn't matter.

Lucid thought came to an end with yet another gruesome discovery. His mind rebelled, and the final threads of his former life broke one by one. He locked away his emotions to sort through them when he could take the luxury.

Anan recognized the end of his second day when the sun's deep red orb rested on the treetops, covering his world in the color of fresh blood. Darkness would come soon and with it the possibility of larger predators. With the clan spell webbing gone, nothing would keep them out.

He knew his duty. He must gather the dead and perform the most sacred of weavings. He would create the final unraveling ceremony for most of the village.

Anan struggled to his feet and began his task. Taking Silbre first, he carried his mate's body to the center of the camp. He ran the back of his fingers over his twining's face, the cold ache of loss constricting around his chest until his breath came in gasps and tears rolled down his cheeks again.

Hesitant at first, Anan carried the remains of each member of his clan and laid them side by side. Lastly he moved to the spellspinners' tents. He understood their importance in the clan, but their aloof manner and vanity over their birthmark velvetless skin had been reason enough for him to avoid them in the past. But his duty was to the village, and his personal disdain had no place. Following the sense of duty hammered into him by his parents, he afforded the spellspinners the same reverence as the other lost.

As he moved toward the final dwelling, and its content, he couldn't help but note the remains of Varas attackers littering the encampment. Some resembled colorless grubs, the sign of a spellspinner calling akhir. The pale Varas bodies also meant there would be a burned spellspinner close by. Akhir extracted a horrible toll. Only in the legends of First Spinner and First Weaver did anyone survive calling akhir.

He grabbed the wrists of a spinner and found the touch of bare skin against his palms... odd. Anan had never touched a spinner before. There had never been a reason to do so. They didn't encourage contact. After steeling himself, he squatted to gather the last of the bodies, when he heard a moan.

Anan spun, knife in hand. When he realized the sound didn't come from attacking Varas, he sheathed his knife and waited, listening for signs of life. A few heartbeats later another barely audible sound leaked from the wreckage. Anan dug through a pile of tent cloth and found a storage cache. Another groan drifted from inside the partially exposed opening, followed by rustling as if a mouse ran across a stretched kuri-skin drum.

Anan eased himself forward, peering into the opening. At first he could see nothing but darkness, but then two brilliant blue eyes peered up at him.

He waited, recognizing the color of a spellspinner's eyes. *How did this spinner survive? Why did he hide?* Compassion returned to Anan. *Regardless of how this spinner survived, he is also Talac.*

"You hurt?" Even to Anan's own ears, his words sounded brittle and desolate of emotion. He waited for a response, but when none came, he reached inside.

"Here. Let me help."

Smooth skin slid under Anan's palms, the first time he'd touched a living spinner. Surprise raced through his system when he found the contact... pleasant. As he helped the slender figure, he recognized this spinner, but not for a reason he might have hoped. The spinner standing before him was the most reclusive. He always avoided contact with any of the Talac who were normal. Who were velveted.

He studied Anan with the suspicion of a young night-hunter, complete with the twitch of his nose. He took the offered hand and scrambled up the side of the cache.

The tension between them grew as their gazes locked. *This isn't about my feelings for the spinners. I must perform the unraveling.* He waited a moment, took in a breath, and calmed himself.

"Can you walk?"

The spinner wiped a grimy arm over his forehead, leaving streaks of filth as he tucked his dark hair behind his ears. An instant later he nodded silently.

"I'm Anan."

This time the young man trembled. "Terja. I am a spinner."

Anan's brow lifted. "Yes. I see you." He considered asking the questions swirling through his mind, but waited.

Terja shuddered again and turned his head slowly. He seemed lost, but Anan granted him time to adjust and waited until the spinner's focus returned. "Where is everyone?"

"Dead. Or taken as Varas slaves. I found only a few bodies from Kuri our age."

Terja's eye's widened. "Slavers? The screams. I heard… it was…." He stared at Anan.

Anan wondered if this spinner still functioned or if the trauma had overwhelmed Terja. Regardless, he continued. "Varas slavers attacked the village. Everyone is either dead or captured. I don't know why the web didn't sound an alert. The herds are scattered. All the Talac clans are in jeopardy."

"Our kuri and herdweavers? Gone?" Terja's voice broke at the news.

Anan stared at him. The herds were the least of his concerns. The herdweavers had either died fighting or were captured. But he knew they hadn't deserted the kuri. They took their role as guardians seriously. But he needed to finish his task, and Terja acted too overwhelmed to help.

Though he moved toward the nearest body, Anan couldn't stop staring at Terja. The irrelevant question wiped out the last of his restraint. "Why were you hiding? The Varas attacked. Why'd you do nothing?"

Tears flooded from Terja's eyes. With his breath coming in gasps, he tried to explain. "I tried. Had my staff. People dying. Father put me—" Terja broke into inconsolable sobbing. Anan knew he would get no more information from the spinner.

"At nightfall we're doing an unraveling for the dead. You're helping."

Terja looked shaken, as if it had never occurred to him a spellweaver would address him in that manner. He began to speak, but when Anan glared at him, Terja pressed his lips tightly together.

Anan motioned to the body of one of the older spinners, and Terja moved to stand at its feet. He clamped his eyes shut as he groped for the ankles, shuddering when the tips of his fingers made contact, and hesitated. Anan allowed him what time he could, but before he had to jar him into motion, Terja clenched his teeth and grabbed the dead man's ankles.

He opened his eyes and glared at Anan, but Anan was far past being affected by anything so minor as the anger of a young spellspinner. With Terja's help, the last bodies were gathered. Exhausted mentally and physically, he still refused to allow Terja to perform any of the ceremony.

"We need to make a final check. It's close to nightfall. I don't want to leave—" Anan stopped and swallowed hard to regain his control. "I want to be certain we've taken care of everyone. We can go opposite directions and meet back here. Hopefully, there's nothing to find."

Anan waited for Terja's nod, then started through the encampment. Hesitant at first, he covered the area with speed and resolve. *I don't know how many more victims I can deal with before my mind snaps like a weak warp thread.* As he worked through the smoldering remains, he began to think they'd recovered all the bodies.

He returned to the center of the encampment and found Terja hadn't arrived. Anan moved to locate the spinner. Close to the spinner's lodges, Anan found him, crumpled into the dust, holding the body of a small child.

His heart cracked when Terja's eyes met his, tears running down his red cheeks. He held the broken body like a precious jewel, cradling the kit who was long past the issues of this world. The spinner ran his fingers over the deep brown velvet covering the kit's face as if he were sleeping. He reached down to touch Terja's shoulder.

"He's gone, Terja. Add him to the ceremony so his strands can rejoin the others in the Great Weaving."

Past reason now, Terja's sobs echoed across the scene of desolation. The darkness flowed over the pair, its edges seeming to ripple in response to Terja's grief. "You don't understand!" he yelled, his face contorted with anger. "Akra and I were friends. His father died when a longtooth pack attacked him. We broke fast together each morning. Why would they kill a kit?"

Anan hardened. "You know why. Akra was nothing more than an animal to them. They don't follow the teachings of First Twining, and we are nothing more than mating slaves to feed their addiction."

"Akra was a sweet kit. Just a toddler."

Anan squeezed his shoulder. "Come. It's time."

He forced Terja into motion. They came to the central area, and Terja turned to Anan. "Clean him. Please. I know it will take some of the spinnings you have, but please. I cannot stand to think he's going to the Great Weaving like this. He worried so much about how he looked."

"Terja...."

"Please. I'll replace the spinning. The spell panels on your kilt are close to full. You have enough matama to do this." Terja turned ashen. "Please. This will be the last thing I ask of you."

Anan sighed and ran his hand over the complex matama patterns stored on his kilt. Although his state of exhaustion diminished his focus to the point where he had to touch the threads. He deftly created the weaving in the air from the matama stored in his kilt panels. Soon he had the simple weave completed. Once he did, Anan struggled through the ritual steps drummed into him to release the spell and clean the lifeless body. The small weaving dissipated, and Anan let his vision slip away.

The kit before them now could have been sleeping. Anan normally would have refused to use a spellweaving on someone beyond its reach, but he admitted, if only to himself, this final visage of the kit was much preferable to the blood- and gore-splattered toddler that had lain before him a short time earlier. He stared at the kit, then at Terja.

"It's time to do the unraveling."

Chapter TWO

The Fitful wind surrounded Anan as he stood among the remains of his friends and family. He reviewed the steps of the spell over and over until the ritual threads were engrained in his memory. Usually the most experienced spellweavers created this final tapestry, but it was one of the first taught when a Talac showed signs of being a spellweaver. Almost any velveted Kuri could do the ritual, one of the few a spellweaver could do without a spellspinner. These final threads were visible to his weaver's sight, large enough that he could weave them. Unlike the threads of matama that only the spinners can work with. Now, as the only weaver left, Anan's web had to be flawless. His stomach knotted and roiled as he moved into position. A slight tremor rippled through him, and he glanced at Terja.

"You stand opposite me and help direct the threads. I know there isn't much you can do at this point. Their matama is gone. But they need the unraveling."

Terja glared at Anan. "I know what an unraveling is. I'm not a child." Without a backward glance, he walked to a point across the bodies from Anan, then stood as unmoving as one of the great southern featherleaf trees.

Anan pulled the needed matama from his kilt and set the weaving in motion. The spell found the fibers of existence and teased them apart in preparation for their release. The Varas had killed these clansmen, and he would avenge them. He focused on his weaving for now, doing his best to ensure their success. He wavered for a heartbeat. *Would they all have died if I'd been here?*

Terja locked his blue eyes on Anan. Focusing only on the task at hand, Anan fought to empty his mind of everything as the last spell threads slid into place. With a twist of the matama, the spell began.

The first shimmering translucent threads slipped from the bodies nearest Anan and drifted into the sky. The mass around them grew thicker as the weaving released more strands and the web began to take shape. The sheer number of threads was overwhelming him as they took on every imaginable color. Time slipped past, and the flurry of threads thickened until he could no longer see Terja.

The air between them filled with threads of being. Anan never recalled an unraveling of this magnitude being performed. The closest he could recall happened a few cycles ago when several herdweavers had been killed in an accident. But then the unraveling was for less than a fingercount of people, and two spellweavers had performed those rites. Anan wasn't certain what might happen with only him creating the unraveling for most of a village. The weavers doing the ceremonies had always been careful to contain the fragments.

A whirlwind of threads finer than a single hair surrounded him, closing off the sky as they crept closer with each passing heartbeat. Shaken to his core, Anan awoke to their impending doom and started to weave. First with the tips of his fingers and gradually invoking larger and more desperate motions as he wove the life threads into a cloth that would carry his people to the Great Weaving. A strangled noise came from Terja and he knew his weave was falling behind the flow of life threads.

His spell vision sharpened as he studied the interweavings for new patterns that would keep them from being overwhelmed. A repeating sequence revealed itself, and Anan added it to his already intricate web. This wasn't a time for subtlety; he needed to weave with more speed and skill than ever before. His hands flew through evolving patterns as the threads came together. The change helped, but the unraveling still threatened to overwhelm the two of them.

Anan used every shred of his hunter-trained muscles to speed his weaving. He hoped his effort would help contain the whirling mass.

Then the first thread touched him, and a tendril of cold shot through his system, twining itself into Anan as it called him to the Great Weaving. Now he understood the cautious methods of his elders.

Anan was losing his fight, but his willpower fueled his efforts. Another fiber slipped around his neck. His throat went numb for an instant, and he struggled to breathe. His hands never slowed, but he knew he couldn't work with this intensity much longer. His growing desperation urged him onward, but his muscles ached, his concentration wavered, and his hands began to slow as he struggled to keep the pattern alive and growing. Anan gritted his teeth and steeled himself for a final attempt.

The fibers began moving slower as if he was mastering the flow. The weaving grew at a phenomenal rate under his flying hands as the lost Kuri were sent into the aether. The threads thinned until he could make out Terja faintly across the space between them. Shock rang through his system at the sight of the younger man spinning the life threads into a larger filament that he was feeding to Anan.

He refocused, working with the thread Terja made. By weaving from the single source he was able to keep up with the flow, and the weaving poured out from his efforts. They worked with more fervor than a pairing with a lifetime of experience. The air around them began to clear, slowly at first and then with increasing speed. As the final fragment of warp thread vanished into the sky, Anan dropped his hands, exhausted and amazed to be alive. Terja stumbled as he made his way across the open space until they were close enough to touch each other. At that point, he began to collapse, his eyes closed.

Anan grabbed Terja as he sagged toward the ground. As he eased the younger man down, he couldn't keep from noting the smooth spellspinner skin. The stain of sweat left dark streaks through Anan's velvet, while water ran in runlets across Terja's body like the tiny hill country streams after a spring downpour. Anan stared at him for a few heartbeats, then swept his gaze across the grounds.

The remains were gone, the blades of grass already beginning to straighten. He turned. "Spinner, what'd you do? With the life threads? They were pulling me into the Great Weaving after I released them. Then you spun thread from the unraveling."

Terja took a deep breath and shook his head. "I don't know what happened. I thought we were going to die. I saw the spirals in the fibers. My teachers always tried to explain them, but I'd never been able to see them before. Poor Pel. He would be so happy I found them." He smiled weakly. "Everything was gone, except for the whirl of colors. So I started spinning the unraveling as if it were deathspinner silk blended with matama. I didn't know what effect I was having. All I could see were the spirals."

Anan stood in slack-jawed disbelief that Terja could spin the life threads. A filament drifted by on the heated evening air. He stared at it for a moment, then walked away without another word. He grabbed his weapons as he strode to the savanna for his final task. As he stalked across the grasslands, the soft shuffling of sandal-covered feet told him Terja followed. Anan's feelings about the spinner were still mixed. But sending his mate as well as most of his village to the beyond left his heart encased by the touch of Iceweaver. The fact that he wasn't certain surviving the unraveling was good left him more unsettled.

As he backtracked his earlier route, Anan came to a small grove, one he'd often used as a playground before he'd gotten his adult velvet. He'd stashed his pack and supplies here to lighten the end of his run, knowing he could retrieve them later, if he survived. He'd known Silbre was dead as soon as their strand broke, even though he'd refused to admit the fact. But he couldn't be certain what else might have been waiting.

In his worst nightmare, he'd never imagined the destruction of the entire village.

Inside the sheltered area, herdweavers had created a cooking pit, but his stomach rebelled at the thought of food. Anger and loss frayed his threads. *Do I want to still live? Is there any reason to try? By First Weaver, it would be easier to curl up like a fatally wounded springtail and let my body shut down.*

"What will happen now?"

He spun at the sound, his knife halfway out, before he remembered Terja. The spinner stood shivering in the warm evening air, and he knew no fire could help Terja's chill. But the light would help beat the darkness into retreat. "Now we start a fire and eat. Tomorrow I will do a bloodweaving. Depending on the Twined One's answer, we will go through the village for anything to help us."

"A vendetta weaving." Terja sighed deeply. "Yes. They must be avenged, and the Varas who did this must be punished. But…."

"Yes?"

"Why did we come out here?"

Anan spread his arms to encompass the grove. "This is a place where I was happy. I couldn't stay in the village any longer. Also, the trees in this grove are placed perfectly to support a web to the Twined Ones."

"So, now…?"

Anan crossed his arms over his chest. "We start a fire and prepare for tomorrow."

CHAPTER THREE

SLEEP HAD been elusive for Terja. His whirlwind of emotions left his stomach in knots and his pulse pounding in his temples. He sat staring into the white ash of their fire.

Anan looked up from his weaving. "What's wrong?"

He shook his head. This wasn't really a conversation he wanted to have with Anan. But the time stretched out until Terja rustled uncomfortably.

"I should have fought. Akra should be alive, and I should be dead if those were the only choices."

Anan sighed and folded his hands in his lap. "I understand. I keep running Silbre's death through my mind again and again. I wonder what would have happened if I'd been here."

"I heard it start. I heard people screaming. I grabbed my staff and ran out in time to see Najal take a crossbow bolt in the chest. I could feel the matama roar through her as she killed the Varas." He looked up as the feelings of guilt and sorrow washed over him. "The smell. That burning smell will haunt me until I join them."

"There are a lot of things that will be with me until I die, too."

Terja squeezed his eyes shut, fighting to keep the tears back. "Did you hide in a hole in the ground while slavers killed a young kit only a few strides away? It all blurs together. Blood, fire, and other things I don't want to think about. I wish my father hadn't hid me away. The guilt of surviving when so many others were killed is a heavy burden."

Anan crumbled a few dry leaves into the fire and silently watched the tendrils of smoke drift for a moment until they burst into flames. "I understand. Maybe we are destined by the Twined Ones to live. But I have no idea why."

15

Terja slumped against the ground. "Why us? Why would they put a spinner and a weaver together? What does that mean? I've always been told—" He glanced over at Anan. "My apologies. It's just...."

Anan's lips formed a tight line as he stared into Terja's eyes. "We know what some spinners think."

Terja dropped his gaze to the fire. After a few moments of silence, Anan returned his focus to creating the vendetta web. Using spell sight he found each color as he needed it and directed the threads from the spell panels into his weaving.

Terja agreed with Anan's decision to create the ritual. But as he studied the weaving, he knew the spell couldn't work. To make the offering whole, Anan needed a spinner to create the threads specific to the ritual. He'd never spun for a bloodweaving, but his training included this bit of rarely used lore. To his knowledge, no one among the Kuri had woven this prayer for generations. The weaving tied the pairing to revenge, or the sacrifice of their lives in the attempt. Creators of this weaving focused on the next breath and no further. Most had few reasons to live past its completion. In the stories told during the season of the Iceweaver, few of the heroes survived. *What do I have to lose? My life is already over. Perhaps we can save some of the captives.*

Anan wove the matama through the night air, creating the spell they needed. He had finished a finger width of the weaving when Terja said, "You're doing it wrong."

Anan tensed, frozen in an instant of time, and then replied, "Spinner, if you can do better or think you have more experience—"

"No one has more experience. You know as well as I do no one has created a bloodweaving for generations. But the weaving takes both a weaver and a spinner. On this subject I am more knowledgeable. I have been training since I could walk."

Anan glared at Terja, the muscles in his jaws tightening. "I've been a spellweaver since my body changed. I might not have the strongest weaves. But by First Weaver, I can declare a bloodweaving!"

Terja knelt beside Anan, reached down, and touched his muscular hand. The wind swirled around them with the scent of heat and endless grasslands. A warmth was shared, surprising Terja with a sensation that died quickly but for a heartbeat left him an odd sense of contentment. "I call vendetta, too. Together we will complete the weaving and avenge the Kuri. There are few enough of us that have more than a thread or two of the ability to see matama."

Anan rocked back on his heels and locked his deep brown eyes with Terja's. He could see the emotions swirling in Anan's eyes. *He fights the same haunting question: Why did I survive?* But Terja's determination grew. Their gazes warred for several moments before Anan shook his head.

"All right, spinner. We will create this weaving to avenge our clan. But I warn you, I will do whatever the Twined Ones ask, including sacrificing both of us."

Terja met Anan's gaze with determination. "Expect the same from me."

Understanding passed between them, and Anan's tense stance lessened. Anan handed Terja the pack filled with supplies he'd gathered during his final pass through the camp. "Eat something, this may take some time. Then you can begin spinning me the other threads you say I need."

They worked steadily, the day slipping past unheeded. Anan wove the complex spell while Terja spun the additional threads needed from their own gathering matama. Anan drew the warp threads tight until each one sang, then began carefully crossing them with threads as he created the sacred pattern. The moon had moved only a short distance in its nightly journey when he put the final binding on the weaving of request. He laid the finished tapestry beside the fire, and the two young men studied each other.

"Now we add our blood."

Without a word, Terja held out his palm and steeled himself. Anan sliced deftly across his hand, leaving a dripping wound. He repeated the action with his own palm. They held their hands over the tapestry, letting their blood mingle into the indecipherable pattern as one of the final elements. Once the last drops splashed across the fibers, they turned to each other.

"Are you prepared for their answer?" Anan asked.

Terja nodded and settled into a comfortable position. He knew the morning sun would provide the final element of their weaving. He expected no sleep this night, and once the spell began, they could wait days for a reply. One didn't petition the gods and expect brevity.

AWAKE SINCE the gray predawn hours, Anan anxiously waited for the sun to break the horizon and provide the final element. As he sat, he renewed their protective web. The scents that remained might attract predators. He did not want to chance them being surprised by a pack of longtooth in the middle of the appeal.

The inner strands of his protective web intertwined with the trees around them to enclose them like a giant egg. As he strengthened the weaving, he considered their situation. His anger had gone from a raging fire to a deep bed of glowing coals. With each breath the scents of their still burning encampment assaulted him. Even if the Twined Ones refused their request, he would track down the slavers. He would not let the killers of the Kuri escape.

Anan added the matama to the web from the spell panels on his kilt. Terja had already performed enough wonders for the past days. He didn't want to abuse their luck by using Terja's spellspinning when there were other ways.

Once Anan finished, he checked each thread of the protection before turning to Terja. "We need to weave our weapon prayers. There should be plenty to make them from inside the web."

Terja began gathering grasses and thin branches from the floor of the glade. Anan collected the delicate branches he needed to create the symbol of his weapon of choice. He twined the strong grasses around each branch, envisioning his weapon. As he worked he began to create a pattern, which pleased him. He tucked in the final strand of grass cordage and glanced over to Terja.

Surprised, he realized they created against tradition. Spellspinners kept peace in the village, while weavers like Anan protected the clan. But he'd created a disc, with full intent of forming a shield, while Terja made the form of a dagger as long as his forearm, longer than the knives of dark metal carried by the Varas.

As the shafts of morning light crept across the waist-high grass surrounding Anan's shelter, the wind quickened and brought the scent of the savanna to him. To the Varas it was featureless wasteland, but the Talac knew the land with the intimacy of a lover. Anan would return that sense of safety to the Talac clans and hoped the Kuri would be among them with the rescue of the captives.

The time came, and the rays of light fell across the bloodweaving. Anan wove the sun into the mesh, and the golden glow flowed from thread to thread until the entire tapestry came to life. A knot formed in Anan's throat as the weaving stretched itself impossibly thin, then disappeared bit by bit. A heartbeat later, the last tendril faded away. "Well, the petition is sent. Hopefully, the Twined Ones will give us our wish."

Anan turned back to strengthening the protective barrier. The familiarity of the task calmed his nerves as they waited. He paused in surprise to see their weapon forms drained of color.

"Anan, what's wrong with the guardian weaving?"

His weaving had thickened until they could see nothing past its opaque walls. He took a step back and studied it. "I don't know. I've never seen a weaving do that before."

Their weapons began to transform as the web grew. Surprised, they watched as the knife lengthened to become one of the sword-clubs of the ancients. As long as Anan's forearm, it was edged with the same sharp obsidian as his dagger. The shield kept its general shape, but jagged pieces of warrior glass grew along its edge as its surface fused into a solid shell.

Anan's gut clenched when the last weft thread slid into place. *The Twined Ones? Already? Should I feel blessed or… terrified?* As the world around them settled into place, vibrations ran up and down the threads like an orb weaver testing its web.

Fear crept into Anan as the weaving surrounding them changed into something more akin to the structure of his blade. No filaments or connections, only a featureless surface. For the first time since deciding to work the bloodweaving, he wondered if they would survive. The impenetrable enclosure thickened with each pulse of his heart until the walls felt as dense as the earth covering a winter lodge. But unlike a lodge, the light continued to grow until the space was brighter than the midsummer sun.

"Twined Ones. What have we done?" Terja asked in an oddly calm voice.

"I don't know. But I don't care. If the Twined Ones kill us, at least that will be an honorable death. I'd rather die with honor than to not try."

The brightness reached a new intensity and began to pulse as if following the beat of some unseen heart. Anan's throat went dry, and his heart raced as he waited. Then he became calm, but he knew it was not of his doing.

He sought out Terja and found him in a relaxed stance, too. But Terja's face was filled with questions. A rustle came from a cluster of branches sealed inside the spellweaving. Nothing could have worked its way past the weaving, not even the smallest crawler. Anan instinctively knew the animal moving closer would never be called small or harmless. The leaves shook violently, and a deathspinner larger than any Anan ever heard of moved down the trunk on eight segmented legs, paused, settled on a branch, and then fixed them with its gaze.

TERJA STUDIED the animal, knowing he should be terrified. Few people, of any race, survived the direct attention of a deathspinner. They were said to trap the soul and will of a person, wrap them in unbreakable silk, and then feed on them for as long as a moon before they finally died. Somehow this horror washed over him, without leaving a trace of fear. All doubt erased, he knew something kept him calm.

Children, are you certain you wish to work at the bloodweaving loom? For some, madness is the only possible result from that warp.

Terja's jaw fell open as the words resonated around and through him, but no sound came through his ears. He glanced at Anan and found the same quality of calm surprise. Their eyes met, and Terja knew he had to address the question.

"Yes, the Varas attacked our village, took people as slaves, and killed the rest. Men, women... and children. The captives must be saved, or the Kuri clan will be no more. The Varas also need to learn what it means to attack the Talac."

The deathspinner tilted its head, appearing lost in thought. Just as Terja decided it would reply, a second, even larger, joined the first. *First Weaver, and First Spinner... the Twined Ones.* Only in the depths of antiquity had both gods appeared together. Even though the calming effect surrounded them, fear slid through Terja's body. He glanced over to see Anan's eyes bulging and his mouth hanging open.

After a few heartbeats of scrutiny, Terja realized the markings of the second creature were curious. Rather than the deep red patterns across their chitin, the base color of the second was the bright yellow of the sunbird and more... rhythmic. A gasp sounded beside him, and he glanced to find Anan's eyes widening.

"What?" asked Terja.

"It's like a history weaving. The last ones in existence were in the safekeeping of the elder weavers. But no one living can read all the symbols."

That's right, weaver child. The second voice echoed through them, unquestionably from a different source. *Some day you may be able to translate the sacred weavings, but today is not that day. You ask for a bloodweaving. For vengeance against these interlopers. First you must understand the meaning.*

To Terja's shock, laughter echoed against him, and he recognized the source from the timbre. The sound came from the first deathspinner. He couldn't see the humor in the moment, but he wasn't one of the gods who oversaw the lands of the Talac. Then he heard and felt the reason for the humor. *Beloved, I believe this would be easier on these two if our forms were less… fatal.*

The two deathspinners scurried from the tree. Once they touched the ground, they began to change and elongate. Terja's eyes watered as he tried to watch the shifting reality of the two forms, but he dropped his gaze and wiped the streaming tears from his eyes. When he could see again, two Talac stood before him. But he had never seen them before.

"Is this form less objectionable, kits?"

Terja blinked, trying to process the sight before him. Their appearance reminded Terja of he and Anan, very similar to how they might look with a few additional years. First Spinner's slender build and hair color could have been Terja's reflection in a calm pool, while First Weaver's masculine body and filigreed facial mask matched Anan almost exactly. The Talac standing before Anan and Terja were dressed in kilts that showed the combined symbols of all the clans, from the Pero to the Meke and all the others. This simply wasn't seen. Their footwear extended to their knees, using a unique intricately woven closure only a senior weaver could open and like nothing Terja had ever seen.

"First Weaver?" came the doubt-filled query from Anan.

The velveted figure smiled. "Yes, I am the latest First Weaver. But we need to share a few things with you. We are not gods, simply the latest holders of the title of First Pairing. The Blessed Ones prefer to not intercede, but we are allowed to assist, when appropriate. Do you understand?"

The young men nodded, the calmness beginning to erode as the visit continued. "So, you are here to help us rescue the captured Talac and avenge the others?" Anan asked.

"Yes. The Blessed Ones agree, the attack must be answered. But there are limits. The formal call for revenge gives you some enhancement of the abilities you already have. Whatever your natural potential, it will be improved. New gifts may appear. Those you will discover as they are needed."

First Spinner took up the instruction. "A bloodweaving will not keep you from death. You are still mortal. Also, in exchange for assistance, you are woven into the bloodweaving until you avenge your village, friends, family, and rescue the Talac taken by the Varas."

"That is our goal, regardless. If the bloodweaving will help, even slightly, then it's a pledge freely given," Anan said.

"Very well. Your weapons have been provided, perhaps not as you envisioned, but as you will need them."

First Weaver again picked up the thread of telling. "Lastly, use caution in who you see as a useful ally and who as a potential enemy. Remember, the fiber is not always true to the spinning."

They tried to take all this in. Amazement filled their faces as First Spinner kissed First Weaver's cheek. He chuckled at the two. "Yes, we are a mezi twining. No, it is not always so, but as I said, we are simply the latest holders of the title."

With that the two slipped back into their deathspinner forms and scuttled up the tree. They disappeared into the canopy, but not without a final warning.

Move quickly, kits. The Varas already attacked the Pero clan. They were not as fortunate as the Kuri. None escaped.

Once First Weaver disappeared, the enhancements to the guard web faded until only Anan's simple weaving remained. Within a few heartbeats, no traces remained of their visit. In spite of the fact their conversation seemed brief, when Anan took down the guardian weaving, the sun was touching the western horizon. He sagged with exhaustion from their trials. But as they checked the glade, they found their requested weapons.

Terja was fixated on a singular piece of information they'd gotten. "The Twined Ones are mezi?"

Anan glanced at him. "So they said, but it doesn't matter. We have other things to deal with. Like what they did with our offering." He motioned to the finished weapons lying in the place of their woven requests.

Terja lifted the weapon fashioned in the place of the simple dagger he'd formed. When he wrapped his fingers around the hilt, he discovered his smaller hand couldn't hold the massive weapon.

"Anan, look."

He glanced at Anan and found him struggling to force his arm into the straps of the shield. The bindings didn't fit any better than the sword fit Terja. He watched for a moment, then motioned for the shield and handed Anan the war club. He studied the disc and then slipped his arm through the straps. The fit was perfect.

He glanced up and found Anan swinging the sword club as if he'd trained with it since he'd come into his powers. "Well, I think these are the first of our surprises. Apparently the Twined Ones thought we needed what the other asked for."

Anan twirled the warrior sword in his hand, the edges a finger thickness from his body. "It does seem… an amazing weapon."

Terja studied the small shield on his arm and ran through some of the ritual movements his father had taught him. The shield sliced through the air. On a whim he touched the rim and yanked back when the edge bit into his flesh. He stood transfixed as blood welled up and began to trickle down his fingers.

Anan lifted the shield carefully from Terja's arm, studied the edge, and found bits of glass woven into the body of the shield.

"It's edged with black warrior glass. Be careful. The Twined One's gift is as dangerous as the sword, even if not as obvious." They both studied their weapons. Each bump and indention seemed to have a purpose, and each fit the wearer perfectly.

As the sun slipped below the horizon, Anan gazed at him. "I think we need rest. You sleep first, and I'll keep watch. The visit of the Twined Ones left me too drained to weave a guardian web. When I get tired, I'll wake you."

Terja stared into the darkness. "I can take first watch. After our visitors today, I'm not particularly tired."

Anan shook his head. "No, go ahead and try to sleep. I need to make plans."

Terja lowered himself to the ground and stared at the deep red moon hanging over them. *Even the moon bleeds for the Talac.*

TERJA STRUGGLED against the brightness of the sun slanting through the deep green palm-sized leaves of the ironwood trees surrounding them. *Wait! Bright? It should be night. What happened?*

He lay without moving and smiled at the soft snoring coming from the form crumpled against the tree. His head rested on a thick kuri-fiber pad Anan must have put under it sometime during the night. As he studied the area with his sight, the new details of the matama made it obvious his spell vision had become stronger. While before Terja's focus would have needed to be perfect to trace a fiber, now the patterns appeared with no effort. Actually, he had to work to avoid seeing the matama thread.

As he lay, a stone began to dig into his hip. He shifted slightly, trying to keep from awakening Anan, but the noise of his movement sounded like a river rock exploding in a hot fire. Before he could draw another breath, the bite of obsidian was against his neck.

"Anan...," he gasped.

Anan snapped from his reflective defense and stumbled backward, almost dropping the warrior blade. "Oh, First Weaver! Terja, I'm so sorry. I almost killed you." He stared at his hands as if they belonged to someone else, disbelief etched on his face. "I've never moved that fast before, and I move quickly. I learned the skill while hunting. But never like that."

"Remember, First Spinner told us some of our abilities would become stronger."

Anan's eyes grew to round discs. "You think my speed came from the gods?"

"Helpers to the gods, and I don't know. But maybe." Terja paused for a moment. "My spell vision seems improved. Have you noticed anything?"

Anan stood unmoving for several heartbeats before turning back. His expression held a mixture of so many emotions Terja couldn't begin to unravel them. "Yes. The matama is bright and easy to see now. It's never been this prominent before."

He sat quietly and then studied Terja for a few heartbeats. Displaying no emotion, he began to speak. "They also said we could die. Whatever has changed, we'll discover. But first we need to check on the herdweavers and their animals. Also, we're going to search the encampment for any food or supplies. We're leaving today, and whatever we can find would help us." He paused again. "Would the spinners have anything hidden away?"

Terja started to deny the unspoken accusation but considered for a few moments. He didn't know everything in the caches. "I'll check." He paused again and then motioned to their kilts. "Did you notice the bloodweaving left us with no matama?"

Anan glanced at his kilt. Yesterday the garment had been covered with dyed threads. Each of the miniature tapestries held the magic he needed for his weavings, but now the carefully woven panels were gone, drained of their stored magic. All that remained was the kuri fabric of their kilts. He looked up, shocked that their reserves of matama were drained. Even with a spinner, the raw matama wouldn't remain for more than a few heartbeats if it wasn't spun with deathspinner silk. Now Anan understood why he couldn't weave the boundary web last night. "We're defenseless. The Firsts have condemned us to death."

Terja took a few breaths, remembering his father's lifeless body he'd helped unravel so recently. "They never said the task would be easy. We're committed to the bloodweaving, or the rips in our life weavings will unravel anyway."

Anan considered his words. "Let's see what we can find."

ANAN WENT through the piles of supplies they had gathered on the square of tent salvaged from their decimated village. They had enough dried foods for a moon. After that, they would either be returning to Kuri lands with the captured clansmen, or dead.

He filled his quiver with a handful of finished arrows. "I'm glad we found the arrowweavers' cache and I could change out my hunting arrows for war arrows."

Terja squatted and ran his finger over the deadly black triangles that tipped each shaft. "Why do we not use metal? The Varas do."

"Iron isn't as sharp as obsidian. Also, a master weaver can unbind it. The old weavers always said iron created more problems, but never shared any details with me."

"Can you unweave iron?"

Anan hesitated and then shook his head. "No, I don't have the ability." He paused for a few moments. "Only a few gifted spellweavers can unravel iron."

"I think we should use iron. The heads would be easier to create and wouldn't shatter."

"No."

There was a sharp glare between them. Anan knew the contest of wills wasted time. But he needed to show the pompous spellspinner who was in charge. He might not have the spinner's birthright of magic, but because it was never a surety, when his spellweaving began to manifest, he'd never been more grateful. The additional work he'd put in to controlling his developing skills had been given with no complaint on his part. Terja wasn't going to slow his progress. Their gazes locked until Terja dropped his eyes. With a sigh he relented. "Fine. No iron."

Without needing more acknowledgments, Anan studied what else they'd found. There were small balls of spellweaving thread in a variety of colors, with healer green dominating. He sorted through the other colors represented in lesser amounts, until he reached the few threads of red. He glanced up and cocked an eyebrow.

"Red is difficult. It comes only from the most violent of emotions, like murderous anger. Spinners become concerned when there is much red to be spun," Terja said.

"You should be able to get plenty of red from me right now."

"Where do you think those threads came from? I harvested them from us and spun them as we traveled."

"The amount is tiny."

"Red is the most powerful color, the most destructive, and most difficult. I hadn't spun rugza threads before. If the slavers were close enough, I might be able to spin from them, but I'm not certain. I do not even know if Varas can be spun. I know of no spellspinner who survived an attack to find out."

Anan traced his finger through the other colored threads, careful to avoid touching the threads of red. As he finished going through the small cache he realized they had a problem. "This silk already has matama spun with it, and it's not enough to reweave our spell panels."

"No, and for what we are about to do our spell panels need to be full. But that will mean a detour, and a puzzle to solve."

"A puzzle?"

"I know where the threads come from but have no idea how to gather them."

"Well, where do they come from? Maybe I can help with how."

"Deathspinner eggs."

He froze in place, then tilted his head toward Terja. "Deathspinner eggs? And how in the pairing are we going to gather deathspinner eggs?"

"I have no idea. I know the fiber comes from what the deathspinners create, and I know the annual harvest is made during this moon. But only the older spellspinners gather them."

Anan filled their pack as he considered the chances of them succeeding. "Then we'll locate the deathspinners and find a way to harvest their silk."

Terja stood silently and then bent to help.

CHAPTER FOUR

GEIR'S COMBAT experience kept him from jumping when the tent flap flew open. He forced himself to wait a heartbeat before fixing a steady gaze at his sergeant, who stood in the open flap.

"It is customary to ask admittance to your captain's quarters."

"Pardons, Geir. But the Talac taken with the last group tried to escape again." A smirk came to the edge of Kotu's lips.

"You don't get him. Execute the slave." Geir's hand tightened on the knife in his belt.

Kotu shot a defiant glare. "You promised me a male. They're nothing more than short furred animals. They don't follow the Red Gods, and this one is already damaged."

The familiar hunger lived in Kotu's expression, and Geir's heart quivered. But he would never let his fear show. "Do as you're commanded, Kotu. It should have never been taken. You know the older Talac are untrainable."

"He was older than I thought. But he would be suitable for what I have in mind. Then I can dispose of him."

He drew his knife and stepped toward Kotu. "Follow my orders. This is the last time you will question me. The slave would have escaped if not for Xain. This one is not yours. Execute him as a lesson to the others. Make certain they see the cost of disobedience."

"As you wish, Geir. Rest assured I'll see to the execution."

He spun to leave the tent when a thought occurred. "Kotu," Geir called.

The underling slowly turned, his body tense and his movement stiff. "Yes?"

"The execution shouldn't last hours."

29

The dark look told Geir his suspicions had been right. Knowing his sergeant likely would try something else, he stood at the tent flap as Kotu stormed to the huddled captives.

He grabbed the dark hair of one of the slaves and yanked him to his feet. Kotu's knife flashed, opening the man's throat, blood spraying over the nearby captives. He held the thrashing body with grim satisfaction until the death throes ended, then dropped the corpse to the ground.

Kotu motioned to two of the other slavers. "Dispose of the carcass. Make sure to take it far enough so it doesn't attract another pack of those meat eaters." He shot Geir a look of disdain before disappearing among the tents.

JOVEN SAT in shock. The abrupt death of the Pero clan member made him want to hide and quiver. He wiped at the blood splattered over him. The drying spots gave him a focus for his overwhelming horror.

A touch no heavier than a feather brought Joven from his thoughts. His glance found the tiny heart-shaped face of one of the other captive Talac and his only friend here.

"They cut his throat like he was a kuri ready for harvest," Morea said in a horrified whisper.

"He was no taller than a Varas. They thought he was an older kit, or he would have been dead when they attacked. The Iceweaver-time stories seem to be true. The Varas are as soulless as they are described." He caught her gaze, surprised to find determination where he'd expected terror and tears.

Morea moved and left bloody prints where she had been standing. As she stepped away, he could see the soles of her feet. He cringed at the raw flesh and her halting gait. He moved to stop her, but his neck ring tightened and pulled him back to the chain binding them all. Trying to get her attention without drawing the Varas to them, he hissed, "Morea."

She stopped and retraced her few steps. "What?"

He nodded toward her feet. "They're getting worse. Let me see them."

She sat beside Joven, and he carefully lifted each foot. "The wounds have opened again. We're going to have to heal the worst of them, or you won't be able to keep up."

Morea checked around them. When her eyes lit on the Varas who'd done this to her, her jaw tightened. "I'd like to have a knife to use on him. I would do more than cut up his feet."

Joven carefully kept his eyes turned downward. "They call him Kotu. Even the Varas seem afraid of him. Don't draw his attention."

"I already drew his attention. How could it be worse?"

"With him, a quick death would be the best you could hope. He was in charge of the attack against the herdweavers. The rest of them died."

"Well, then, I'll hope it's quick. Because I'm not going to get better."

Joven glanced at the spell panel on his kilt. For some reason the matama faded a little each day. But he thought enough existed for his needs. "Morea, let me see."

"You can't. It's forbidden! If we give away the secret of the Talac we could lose the gifts."

He glanced around, wondering if anyone would notice if he healed some of the damage. Their guards seemed convinced they were cowed and paid them little attention.

"Morea, I only have a few threads left, but my healing weavings are usually good. If the weavers could use akhir…."

"Then we would all be dead. Besides, the Twined Ones blocked akhir for us. You know as well as I that spellweavers' magic is for healing and protecting the clan. We cannot use our spellweavings to harm someone. Otherwise the Varas would have taken none of us."

He shook his head and gave Morea a feral smile. "I can wish, can't I? Even if I am the coward who surrendered to the Varas."

She laid her hand on his arm. "You're still alive. You weren't a coward. The gods spared you for a reason."

Joven pressed his lips together. "The Varas think the spinners do our healing. They'd never catch me so long as I do it a little at a time. I have to try before whatever is draining the weaving panels takes the last of it."

He took Morea's feet in his hands and began rubbing them, hoping to hide his actual purpose. For years he'd struggled to pull the matama from spell panels without touching them. If he couldn't succeed this time, Morea's remains would be longtooth food, too.

Joven kept the surprise from his expression when a trickle of healing flowed from his fingers at his attempt. As he continued to rub Morea's soles, the matama weavings formed in his spell sight and settled over the wounds. The threads moved over her feet for a moment before Morea pulled them from his hands and shook her head.

She leaned close, nodded to the man towering over the Varas he stood with, and whispered, "The traitor is watching us. He can't see you healing me. Besides, if you heal them too much the guards might notice."

Morea was right. He couldn't heal her completely, or the Varas would discover their secret. She stood again and walked with care to the waterskin. She drank from it before settling to the ground opposite Joven. They'd both learned the lash marks were fewer if the Varas didn't think you had friends among the other Talac.

Once their guards moved away, Morea eased herself beside Joven. The Varas ate their evening meal. The scarcity of food left the captives hungry enough that even the wretched smell of the foul Varas cooking enticed him. But they would get no food from that quarter. The Varas wanted the captives weak.

Morea moved behind him. He enjoyed the companionable touch as her body pressed against his back.

"Sleep well, little one."

"I just pray to First Weaver that we wake up to find out this is all a horrible nightmare."

"Yes, I'd like to awaken from this horror, too."

JOVEN SCREAMED as the fire of the lash burned across his cheek, awakening him. He fought his confusion in the faint predawn light and recoiled in agony when the lash cut into his chest. He bit back a cry, unwilling to give his tormenter the satisfaction of a second reaction. He knew who wielded the whip. Joven learned early in his captivity to fear the bite of Kotu's braided leather serpent and to hate the expression of pleasure that filled the man each morning when he woke the prisoners.

He pulled Morea up, clamping his teeth together to hold in the gasp of pain when a third strike landed over an already bleeding wound and the stream of blood running down his velvet grew heavier. Kotu moved down the line, cries of pain from other captives announcing his presence.

The prisoners formed a line as they did each morning, and the Varas flanked them, crossbows cocked and ready. Joven made an almost invisible gesture toward Morea.

"They're arming themselves more than usual. They're worried our longbows will find them before they can slither back to their river," Joven said.

"We're close to the edge of the Talac lands?"

"Not that close. It will take most of a moon. The injured are slowing us down, too. But there might be more Talac encampments between the Varas lands and us. Hopefully the foothills will slow them. I'm sure someone will come."

She didn't meet Joven's gaze. "I don't think there's anyone left."

His gut knotted at her words, but before he could reply, the whips cracked above the huddled group, signaling them to move. Joven shuffled along, careful to keep slack between others chained in front and behind him. He looked down to find Morea walking beside him.

"I don't think they'll let you stay with me."

She began to reply when she tripped and almost fell. Standing, she took a step and cried out in pain. Morea shot Joven a panicked expression. "The cuts tore open."

Before either of them could utter another word, a lash cracked, and searing pain shot across his back. He jerked backward to find Kotu spinning his whip for a second strike. Their eyes met, and he let the lash settle, then began recoiling the braided leather.

"The female is damaged and can't keep up. Kill her," Kotu said.

He motioned toward two of the muscular bearded soldiers, who started for Morea, and Joven moved to stand in front of her. "I'll carry her."

Kotu's smile broadened as he released his lash. To worsen the situation, the twisted matama of lust coming from the two guards was thick enough for Joven to sense. Kotu chose them because they would enjoy themselves before killing Morea. *I won't let them take her without a fight.*

"If he'll carry her, let him. She's worth much more alive than dead."

Joven spun to find the expressionless captain staring at him. Then he glanced toward Kotu and could almost taste the hatred and frustration streaming from the man. He had made an enemy, a dangerous enemy.

"And if he doesn't?" Kotu's face contorted with anger.

"Then kill them both." Geir turned to leave, then glared at Kotu. "Don't spend the day cutting them with your whip either. If they fail through your fault, I'll send you to the pleasure stables to compensate my loss."

Kotu's face reddened, but he nodded. His fists clenched and unclenched, the flow of blood red matama so thick Joven wished they had a spinner to harvest the threads. He stood still for a heartbeat before crouching to let Morea clamber onto his back. The fresh cuts bled freely as she pressed against them, but nothing could be done other than hope the gashes would close on their own.

Morea settled into place and, with her lips a hairsbreadth from his ear, whispered, "Thank you, Joven. You're very brave."

CHAPTER FIVE

THE PAIR worked their way through the foothills filled with towering trees and patches of dense brush, closing the distance to the colony. Terja had recalled the location of the deathspinners from overhearing the elders' conversation. They both were focused on their goal of rescuing the captives and avenging their families. He knew Terja ached as much as Anan did for Silbre.

The day was drawing to an end when Anan paused and studied their surroundings.

"What?" Terja asked.

"I'm not sure. It's like the velvet on the back of my neck is standing on end." Anan struggled to identify the source of his unease.

After another wave of sensation, this one verging on painful, he grabbed Terja's shoulder. The two travelers froze. Anan listened intently but heard nothing. *I wonder....* Anan wove a loose version of a guardian web, only this one he sent through the surrounding grasslands, asking the waist-high grass what it hid. To his surprise it did exactly as he hoped and told him of nothing more threatening than a family of springtail. The weaving stretched close to the limits of Anan's spell when he found what he'd hoped to avoid—a hunting pack of longtooth.

"Longtooth. Only a hill or two behind us."

Color drained from Terja's face. "On our trail?"

"Can't tell. Move. We don't have enough matama in the new spell panels to hold off a pack." Anan pulled his bow from his shoulder and nocked an arrow. Moving at a lope, he scanned for a place where they could defend themselves. Having moved beyond the treeless Kuri grasslands gave the pair choices they wouldn't have had otherwise. But the longtooth's retractable claws allowed the large predators to climb. This meant any protection had to cover them from all sides, including above. He berated himself for keeping his distance from Terja rather than working together to replenish their spell panels.

Anan left the tracker web in place. From the pace of the longtooth, he knew the pack scented them. He and Terja ran faster, searching for a place they could stop and face the animals. He'd heard of packs with as many as thirty. He tugged at the threads of his weaving, trying to get an idea of the size of this pack. The results chilled him.

There was a small hope. The colony of deathspinners they were trying to find made their home in the rough hills marking the Talac's southern border. The steep ravines and blind canyons Anan and Terja ran through gave them a chance of finding a defensible stopping place. If the longtooth had discovered them on the open grasslands, there would have been no hope.

Terja skidded to a halt. Anan bit back his frustration, thinking he was already winded, when the spinner pointed to a recent rockslide covering one wall of the small canyon. "There. Cave," he managed to gasp out. Anan gazed intently, then sprinted toward the rocks.

The shelter consisted of little more than a shallow dish in the hillside, but it was better than being caught by the longtooth pack on open ground. The tone of the pack's hunting howls changed as they sensed their prey fleeing and rippled over the hill behind them. Their ear tufts were tucked tight against their skulls, and their long tails swung behind them as a counterbalance to the coiling and uncoiling of their bodies as they raced to overtake their prey.

Anan heard their hissing calls as the longtooth closed in on them. He spun, drew an arrow to his cheek, and released at the closest animal. The shaft leapt from Anan's longbow, and then he raced to follow Terja. Behind him a longtooth's death scream filled the air as his arrow found its mark.

He sprinted closer to the shelter, surprised to find Terja standing ready, his pair-gifted shield on one arm and a sling in the other hand. Anan recognized the sling as the weapon used by the herdweavers. He'd noticed it with Terja's gear their first night together. The sounds of the pack moved ever closer as Anan focused on the scramble into the cave.

Terja snapped the sling forward, and a howl of pain came from the nearest longtooth. As Terja sent a second deadly missile into the pack, Anan moved into the opening, nocked an arrow, and searched for a target. To his surprise, he found the pack at bay, with three dead.

The beasts paced back and forth, their furry tails twitching like the branch of a featherleaf tree in a summer storm. Anan had heard descriptions of these animals since he was young, but he couldn't keep from noting the glimmer from the two long teeth protruding far past the bottom jaw. They paced a safe distance away, cutting off any possible avenue of escape. Anan's breathing started to calm, when the longtooth charged them again. Anan loosed three arrows in rapid succession, cutting the size of the pack by the same count. From Anan's quick check, Terja brought down an equal number before the predators retreated again. This time he gave Anan a grim smile.

"The herdweavers taught me well. They would be pleased."

"Very well. They are in my debt. You've taken out more of the longtooth than I have."

"Unfortunately, I don't have many pellets left."

Anan glanced upward just as a snarling longtooth jumped from above. He swung his bow as Terja's shield sliced through the air. The edge of obsidian severed skin and sinew as if it were air. The animal clawed frantically as it died, leaving Terja with a deep gash across his arm.

He moved to stop the bleeding, but Terja motioned him away. "It won't kill me, at least not as fast as they will. I can't use the sling now. You have to see what you can weave, or nothing else will matter."

Anan drained the last matama from their kilts and began. His sight slipped into place without conscious thought, and he sent the first warp threads arching over their heads. As thick as his ironwood bow, they would withstand a night of guardianship, if he could create a weft of equal strength. The horizontal strands were slower in forming, and Anan could tell they didn't have enough in the spell panels to finish what he'd started.

Anan put his hand on Terja's shoulder, expecting to share a final good-bye, when a surge of matama ran up his arm and into his weaving. He stared at the spinner, shocked as the impossible happened again. Terja was feeding the spun matama from the two of them directly to Anan. He had no idea how he was accomplishing the feat. But he was. When the longtooth surged toward them, he knew a discussion about what just happened would have to wait until another time.

By lucky accident, or with the help of the Twined Ones, trees large enough to support the defense they needed surrounded them. Although with the amount of energy Terja was channeling into Anan, he felt as if he could rebuild their entire village on force of will alone. Anan glanced at him and saw the toll. Terja's face had drained of color as he fed all the matama he could gather to Anan. Horrified, he yanked his hand away and broke the connection. Terja staggered, his arm coated in his own blood and his face the color of death.

Forced to trust his weaving to hold against the hissing animals a handsbreadth away, Anan wove a healing and cast it over Terja's wound. He discovered the injury was much deeper than Terja had let Anan believe. As the bleeding stopped, he could see white bone.

Careful not to take any more matama from Terja, he used the last healing fibers. The threads of green flowed through torn muscle and veins, binding them together. Anan repaired the most severe of the injuries but left the others, knowing Terja's natural healing would deal with those. Once he finished, his exhaustion extended to the depths of his soul.

He pulled Terja against his side and leaned on the dirt wall at the back of their shallow cave. In one hand he held his war club and in the other, Terja's shield. The longtooth paced the edge of the spell, testing the walls occasionally as Anan waited, hoping the weaving held. But as Terja slept, the healing web finished releasing its magic. Anan braced himself, ready to do what he could if the weaving failed.

The sun flitted through the branches and woke Anan. He lurched to his feet, ready to do battle, only to find them alone. Terja sat beside him, the color returning to his face. They scanned the canyon and found no sign of the pack.

He turned to Terja and lifted a brow. "Lots of surprises last night."

TERJA FILLED with awe at the sight before him. They had traveled for more than a handcount of days from the Kuri village, but nothing they'd seen had prepared him. Translucent sheets covered the trees of the small valley. In the reflected light of the setting sun, they took on the colors of fire, creating the imagery of a slow-moving blaze. Tiers of gossamer membranes covered the ground, fluttering in the light breeze, further enhancing the illusion.

"That's a deathspinner web?" Anan asked.

Terja knew it really wasn't a question. No other creatures could cover the landscape with their work. The hair on Terja's neck rose, and he could swear Anan grew slightly in size as his velvet stood on end. Something about viewing the work of the most lethal predator in the Talac lands made the danger even more real.

"These are not avatars of the Blessed Ones."

Terja glared at Anan. "I know. I'm not slow-witted." He glanced across the valley, and a shiver ran up his spine. "I'm not certain I could have stood here if the Twined Ones hadn't appeared to us in the guise of a deathspinner."

A crash came from the lower valley, followed by the intense hissing of a pack of longtooth coursing prey. Anan stepped in front of him and swept him backward with a motion of his arm. He moved with fluid grace, his loaded bow seeming to jump to his hand.

An odd sensation flowed through him too quickly to be cataloged as Terja armed himself as well. He raised the glass-edged shield, and his muscles responded as if he'd trained with it for a lifetime. His injured arm tucked against his chest, Terja let his spinner's vision shift into being. As he studied the webbing in front of him, he realized their uniqueness. He could detect no beginnings or endings, just a mat of fibers radiating in all directions. He began to take in the information when the prey of the longtooth pack topped the ridge opposite them. Even from where they stood, the flaring nostrils of the terrified daggerhorn buck were clear. Blood stained its hindquarters from four ragged slashes. The animal snorted, its eyes bulging at the sight of the valley of webs.

Both men sat immobile, their breathing shallow as the tableau played out before them. The daggerhorn's squeals of terror filled the valley. Cornered, the panicked animal spun and raked one of the longtooth with its horns. The air rippled with an ear-splitting scream of pain as the daggerhorn's poison flooded the longtooth. The predatory figure curled into itself, then snapped open in a bone-breaking convulsion that pitched it down the hillside.

He started to move, needing to take action, when Anan rested his hand on Terja's shoulder. "No. Watch."

The longtooth's death throes pitched the body onto the outermost webbing. Terja saw the web move toward the dying animal. "It's growing...."

"Yes. Faster than my teachers described."

Shrouds of webbing engulfed the longtooth, and the nearest of the fist-sized multilegged creatures raced to their prey. The deathspinners converged, but this time their haste wasn't warranted. The daggerhorn poison had worked with lethal efficiency.

"The longtooth was lucky."

Terja twisted his head, certain his face echoed his disbelief. "How could you think that?"

"Daggerhorn poison is fast, if painful. Caught alive inside of a deathspinner colony is... I wouldn't even wish them on the Varas. They inject their venom, and the poison melts you inside. Then they feed."

"They both sound horrible."

"Old tales tell of deathspinners keeping a victim alive for an entire moon."

"First Spinner, protect us," Terja muttered.

Anan paused for a moment and then continued. "The victim's alive but can't move while they eat your dissolving flesh. Nothing could be worse."

Anan motioned with his bow to the ridge where the drama had unfolded. "That daggerhorn's wounded, and a hungry pack of longtooth are close. Tonight we'll need to be especially careful."

"What do you suggest?" Terja asked.

"We eat, rest, and then figure out how to steal the silk from something that's walking death."

"We're making camp?" He glanced to the dead longtooth, whose body was covered by deathspinners.

"Not here. Neither of us will rest if we stay this close. The last stream we crossed should be a safe distance. It'll be easy to weave a guard web to protect us for a night."

Terja glanced back and stood stunned as the creatures flowed from the webs until the ground for several paces around the carcass was covered. A shiver ran through him. Somehow they had to solve the puzzle of how to steal from the most poisonous animal on the savanna. Everything needed to happen in the next day, or they would only be performing unraveling for Talac lucky enough to be killed before being sold.

"Yes, making camp away from this valley would increase my chances of sleeping. I'll search through the history weavings. Maybe this new sight from First Spinner will help me identify the glyphs spellspinners haven't been able to unravel before. I hope something in them will help."

Anan stared at Terja for a few moments but said nothing. Instead he retraced their path to the stream they'd crossed earlier. The sun stood only a short distance past midday, but neither of them wanted to be unprotected after being attacked by the longtooth pack.

In a short time, they reached the site. It was close to perfect, with a small level area for sleeping and surrounded by northern featherleaf trees that shaded them from the fierce sun. Terja tasted the water. *Sweet and cold. Thank the Twined Ones.* In the heat of midsummer, and with dried foods to sustain them, they didn't need a fire.

They laid out a scrap of tent as a ground cloth, and Anan began his protective weaving. But only a heartbeat passed before he stopped and stared at Terja helplessly.

"I forgot. We used all the matama. Do you think you could spin more from us like you did with the longtooth?"

Terja shook his head slowly. "From what? We've both exhausted our spell panels, and we are so tired that there is almost no matama."

Pulling himself from the morass, Terja studied the problem, trying to find a solution. He ran through his lessons, tales of the old ways, anything that might give them a clue of how to protect themselves. He distantly recalled a way to create a barrier… but of what? Then the obvious solution came to him.

"Guardian bushes. We can make the barrier out of them," Terja said.

Anan stared at him with an expression of disbelief. "Guardian bushes? With poisonous thorns as long as my hand? Those guardian bushes?"

Terja waved his hand at Anan, dismissing his skepticism. "They are woven into walls. We can do it. But it may be the most careful weaving you've ever done."

Anan lifted his brows and stared at Terja. "If you think so. I don't have a better idea. Does every solution to our problem need to have a deadly poison? Never mind, I don't really want to know. I think I recall some of the bushes fairly close."

The sun had barely moved when they returned, dragging several large bushes. With great care they began to weave the lethal thorns through the dense branches. A few hours later they had created a thin wall bristling with thorns on the outward facing side. Anan created a portal to put in place once they finished for the evening and then stepped back to gauge their shelter. "I think this will work."

"Anything that challenges those thorns will wish they hadn't."

With the barrier completed, they readied for another night. Terja brought out the history weavings, knowing time to find a solution was running out. As he scanned them, Anan went through his pack and pulled out several pieces of dried meat for them to share.

Anan gripped a corner with his strong white teeth, worried a bite free, and began chewing. He gnawed at the leather-tough piece of dried kuri as he stared at the area surrounding them. The silence stretched out until it became uncomfortable before he swallowed and glanced at Terja. "Have you found a way to get the eggs?"

Terja shook his head as he studied the weavings before him. "No, nothing. Some nonsense about getting the deathspinners away from the webs and taking only certain eggs. It doesn't even sound like they're really eggs. Their glyph is a little different. But which eggs, and how to get them away...." Terja's stomach knotted with the worry that he wasn't up to this task.

Anan swallowed the bite of food and lay on the ground cloth. "Get some rest. Hopefully tomorrow things will come together."

Terja stared at Anan for a few moments, then lay beside him. His skin brushed against Anan's velvet, and he gasped at the wave of heat through his body. He tensed and admonished himself. He would not become one of the spinners paired with a weaver. Such a coupling was an anathema to the spinners; his father had told him so again and again.

ANAN SHIFTED in Terja's arms as he awakened in their camp the next morning, and he released the weaver. He wasn't certain why he'd embraced him. But somehow, when he'd sensed a shudder, Terja understood the emotional turmoil.

They separated, and Anan sat for a moment before turning to Terja. His cold expression was unchanged. Terja recognized the stony glance as he fought his own battle to keep from being overwhelmed. The difference? Now the emotionless gaze was locked on him.

"How do we get the eggs?" Anan asked.

Terja took a deep breath to prepare himself. "I've studied the old weavings, taking what each of us can read from the glyphs, but the instructions make no sense."

"Tell me what it says. Maybe I can help."

Terja unrolled one of the palm-sized tapestries and traced over the pattern. To someone without spell vision, he simply held one of the bright miniature weavings created by the Talac. But when they let their vision flow into existence, new patterns arose. "It's obvious you must not kill a deathspinner. The weaving doesn't really say why, but there is no doubt it's forbidden."

"All right. Then how're we doing this?"

Terja ran his fingers through his hair. "This is where the writing gets confusing. It says you kill them."

"What?"

"Here. That's the glyph for death, but it is a variation I've never seen before."

Anan looked at the weaving, and his lips twitched. "The symbol doesn't say death, it says little death."

"What's the difference?"

For the first time since they'd met, Anan smiled. He wasn't certain how happy he should be about Anan's shift in mood.

"Weavers call the corcra threads of matama—little death. The purple threads of passion, those strands are harvested from…."

Hot embarrassment flashed across Terja's face. "Those are intimacy threads. Only twined pairs give off corcra, and it's forbidden to gather those."

"It's forbidden to harvest them from someone else, but not your own pairing. When the spellspinners harvest silk, do they go in pairs?"

The heat intensified in Terja, and he desperately wanted this conversation to end. "Yes, only one pair at a time. At least a few days apart."

"Then I'd guess they're making corcra thread while they're here." Anan paused and studied their campsite more carefully.

"This clearing isn't natural. My guess is they stay here. Check for corcra fibers."

Without comment, Terja began to carefully scan the area around them with his sight. Focusing closer and closer, he found fragments of corcra. A bit here and a smidge there, almost too tiny to see even with his enhanced sight, but undeniably present. And corcra only came from the mating of twined pairs. At the thought of what happened in this tiny clearing, Terja's face burned until it seemed he could light a blaze.

"Yes, close to invisible, but I found bits of corcra. That means they were here recently. Corcra fades away quickly, and these are almost gone. The last pair to come must have been just before...." Terja stopped, not wanting to recall memories for either of them.

"So, a corcra weaving puts them to sleep."

"We think that's what happens. But do you know the weaving patterns?"

Anan looked away, unable to meet Terja's gaze. "I know the weave. Silbre and I generated plenty of corcra during our time together and wove patterns for our own fun. But without a spinner they faded as quickly as they're woven.

"We need the corcra matama. And corcra only comes from mating...."

Terja shook his head and turned away. "No, we aren't twined. And—"

"And your pairing match is a woman. You're nisa. It would be against the will of the Twined Ones to force someone into an unnatural mating."

"I'm mezi. I'd choose a male for my pairing. But...."

Terja refused to meet Anan's eyes. Several heartbeats passed before understanding spread across Anan's face.

"You've never been with anyone."

Terja's chest contracted, and his mouth went as dry as the grasses before a fire wind. "Yes. Are you satisfied now? I claim mezi, but I've never given myself to anyone."

Anan inhaled deeply and then let it out slowly. "I'm sorry."

"Why? You've done nothing wrong."

"Your first time should be special and with a lover if not a twining. I wish there was some other way."

"No! I won't! Especially not with a hair-covered weaver." Panic surged through Terja. Unable to find an alternative, he turned on Anan like a trapped daggerhorn. "I won't, I...."

His mouth opened and closed several times as he struggled to form rational thoughts. He remembered the early-morning touches and the threads of pleasure that wove through him at the touch of the weaver's velvety covering. Regardless, he couldn't forsake the sacred vow of twining. Anan should still be in mourning, too. He met his eyes and began to speak, but as if reading his mind, Anan cut him off.

"None of this should be happening, Terja. I should have time to mourn. We should have time to mourn. Traditions hold power, but I will save the Talac they took or die trying. Silbre would understand. He would do the same. This is when the Paired Ones will understand when we don't follow the weaving of tradition so exactly." He turned his back to Terja, his body tense and his arms crossed.

His words slipped through Terja, finding similar wounds. *My father's death should have me struggling too. Why am I not?* As much as Terja's emotions roiled and twisted, he agreed. They had to rescue the captured Talac.

"We aren't twined. Would our matama even form corcra?" Terja asked.

Anan shrugged, still facing away. "I don't know. But there aren't any other choices."

He swallowed hard and nodded before realizing Anan couldn't see him. "Yes. I agree. I see no other choices."

Anan stepped close and cupped Terja's face gently. He wore a regretful smile when their eyes met. "I'm sorry. Maybe if you close your eyes and think of someone you find attractive this won't be so unpleasant."

After taking Anan's measure, Terja sighed in resignation, freezing in place as they eased closer. His breath came in gasps as the inevitable touch loomed. Anan's caress made him aware of how sensual a simple touch could be. The flutter of warm breath drifted across his lips, a faintly pleasant scent curled into his nostrils, and Terja shuddered.

Their lips touched, and a flash of fire shot through him. Terja stiffened under his kilt. The already wonderful sensations intensified at the nip Anan gave his lip as they separated. He studied Terja carefully, then let out his breath.

"Does it work?" Anan asked.

Terja blinked and then stared at the filaments of every shade of purple that swam around them. He could never remember seeing threads of a color so thick. He swallowed hard, his legs barely able to hold him upright.

The fog of pleasure lifted as he considered his answer. "If we're forced, I could gather some corcra. Let's study the animals today. Maybe the weavings have another meaning."

Without a word, Anan began to prepare for a day of deadly stalking.

CHAPTER SIX

THE SUN had dipped back into the west when they returned from studying the deathspinners. Terja dropped to the ground at their camp and exhaled noisily. "They took down a springtail today just like they did the longtooth. The webs are so thick the prey can't get away."

Anan lifted the bow and quiver from his shoulder and laid them within arm's reach. "They move faster than I expected. And the webs seem to have a life of their own. I guess I wasted the two arrows today killing the animals they'd trapped, but I just couldn't let them suffer."

Terja shook his head in disbelief. "It was as if the springtail couldn't even see the webs until they were trapped. That is frightening to consider. We can't get to the eggs. You saw how fast they took down the springtail, and their eggs have to be in the densest part of the web. It would be impossible to use speed."

"Yes."

"The deathspinners knew the minute the animals tangled in their web. We can't sneak up on them."

"No. And even if we were able to distract the deathspinners, we'd be helplessly entangled after only a few steps."

Terja sighed with resignation. He knew his duty. No matter how he felt about Anan, he would harvest the matama. After what he lived through during the attack on their village, sharing intimacies was a small sacrifice. He met Anan's gaze. "All right. Let's make the corcra. Hopefully the solution to traversing the web will appear too."

Anan smiled thoughtfully. "Creating corcra isn't a death sentence, Terja. Most people even consider it pleasant." His voice caught slightly. "It certainly was with Silbre."

His glare was the distillation of Terja's building emotions. "With my choice of partners, in my chosen place, then it's pleasure. This is duty. I swore revenge. I'm sure this will be far from the greatest sacrifice I'm asked to give." His gaze dropped, and he lowered his voice. "First Twining was clear; there's never a bloodweaving without personal sacrifice."

Anan sat beside Terja and caressed his bare arm. Surprised, Terja realized he didn't find the touch unpleasant. Quite the opposite, actually. A warmth spun through him at the touch. He met Anan's gaze and found himself lost in his deep brown eyes. The darker patterns coiling across Anan's face drew Terja closer.

"I can make the experience comfortable, even if it's not what you'd wanted," Anan said.

"I know."

Anan frowned slightly but didn't comment further. He dragged their packs close and pulled out more trail rations for their evening meal. After dividing the sparse food between them, he sat and chewed while he stared into the growing darkness.

With the heat of the sun still filling the air, Terja felt no need to wear more than his kilt. A cooling breeze blew across his torso like a lover's caress. His gaze drifted over a silent Anan. *He's not unbecoming.* A typical weaver with thick arms and thighs, attractive if you prefer that sort. His beautifully marked velvet formed dark patterns of swirls from his cheeks to his belly and chest. His shoulders and back were a shade of rich brown. Slightly taller than Terja, he would tower over most Talac. He moved with the grace of a mating longtooth, all power and—lust. But he was still a weaver, a furry spellweaver. Spinners mated only with other spinners. His father had made that clear. Mezi or not, Terja could do better than the velvety-covered spellweavers for a mate. But what they did here had little to do with him selecting a twining.

Anan glanced back, the last light of the sun reflecting off his dark brown eyes. He finished the last bite of travel food, wiped his hands on his kilt, and then moved close. At his touch, Terja tensed.

Anan leaned close to Terja's ear and whispered, "Relax. I promise. It won't be as bad as you think."

He ran his hands over Terja's smooth skin, the soft touch creating a summer storm of lightning. Like everyone else, he'd played grownup with his friends when he was a kit. Kissing, touching, and rubbing against each other, trying to copy the intimate moments of the adults around them. But this? The pressure building inside was as similar to those childhood fumblings as the little orb weaver was to a deathspinner. He moved over Terja's chest, his work-roughened palms leaving him panting. As his thoughts merged with his growing arousal, Terja remembered their goal and lunged away. He stood gasping for breath in the cooling night air.

Concern and anguish were written across Anan's face. "What's wrong, Terja?"

He managed to gasp out. "Silk. No silk for the corcra."

Anan smiled gently. "I guess that was the whole reason."

Terja found his pack and dug through the contents. He located a carefully folded pouch and pulled out the small set of prepared fibers. He sorted through them for a moment before glancing at Anan with a horrified expression.

"We don't have any blank deathspinner silk. We can't save the corcra. It has the shortest life, in a few eye blinks the useable matama will be gone."

Anan slipped the spinner kit from Terja's grasp, searched through the orderly arrangement and pulled out the mistakes, making Terja cringe. "What possible use are those? I'm not even sure why I kept them. My work is typically of higher quality."

Anan teased the almost perfect threads apart. "It's good fiber. We can use it for the corcra."

He stared at Anan as if the days since the attack had left him damaged. "You would need to burn out the weaving. When you pull the matama it destroys the silk."

"Yes. I know how the spells work. But good weavers have a way to clean unused silk."

Anan unwound the threads, then began braiding a spell panel no wider than his smallest finger. The colors marbled and muddied in ways Terja had never seen with a weaving. The sight made his vision swim until he glanced away to steady his stomach. When he looked back, Anan displayed a small woven piece on his palm.

Terja settled his spell vision into place, and he could see the matama shift and strain, frantically trying to escape. He smiled at their lifelike antics. After a few moments he glanced up and fell helpless into Anan's gaze. Dropping his stare, Terja struggled to control his emotions that swirled and fought as much as the weaving.

"It's as if they are trying to escape each other."

Anan returned the smile and nodded in agreement. "Well, I basically told them they didn't like each other. The matama will go into the aether and leave the silk almost like new."

A rainbow of matama escaped the weaving as Terja watched. A few breaths later the band emerged close to the same white as the day it was harvested. Anan carefully unraveled the tapestry and presented the threads to Terja. He took Terja's hand inside his own and gently closed his grasp around the threads. He kissed Terja lightly on the cheek and ran a fingertip along the underside of his wrist. Terja's pulse raced.

"I think you can store whatever corcra we create into these," Anan said.

Terja studied the fiber for a moment. It wasn't new, but it would work. A bit of Anan lingered in the material, drawing him to the larger man. He sensed the thoughtful expression and remembered their goal. Their gazes met as Anan moved closer and let his thumb trail along the edge of Terja's jaw.

The touch of his work-roughened skin ignited a fire in Terja. Pulled by the heat of their contact, he caressed the weaver's forearm. *Strands, why would this be forbidden?* The fine hair created sensations more pleasant than the most intricate weavings he had ever touched. To the eye, the short dense velvet could be seen only as a slight softening of Anan's features, but touching it made Terja unwilling to ever release his hold.

Anan pressed their lips together in a tender kiss. The wildfire coursing through Terja raged stronger than ever before. His heart pounded as jolts of lightning shot from his lips through the rest of his body. He groaned when his hardening cock pressed against the thick material of his kilt. His pleasure deepened as its sensitive crown rubbed across the textured fabric.

Their kiss became more urgent, fueling the building heat inside Terja. Part of him wanted to run, to escape Anan and the confusing emotions he kindled. But another portion of his mind wanted more. What more consisted of—he wasn't certain. Time stretched until the fire burning in him roared with intensity.

Anan broke the kiss. "You all right? I'm sorry your first time has to be like this. If we had any choice...."

The last sparks faded from his system. Confusion warred with lust. "No. It's all right. We must do this."

Anan whispered, "Remember, relax."

Terja struggled to keep a giggle from escaping. He kept reminding himself that spinners shouldn't mate with weavers, but the feelings of pleasure curling through him made it difficult to believe. Right now, he would be content rubbing against Anan and forgetting the past handful of days.

Anan spread his powerful hand across Terja's chest and eased it downward until it slipped along the top of the kilt. Terja shuddered as his touch lingered playfully on the line of hair creating a trail from his navel to disappear under his clothing. Anan flicked the tip of his tongue along the side of Terja's neck and then whispered, "You spinners have hair in the oddest places."

The scent curling through Terja left him trembling. He ran his shaking hands over Anan's arm, then trailed them over the hillocks of muscle forming his shoulders. "While you weavers have hair everywhere."

He slid his finger down the bridge of Terja's nose. "Not on my palms, the bottoms of my feet, or...." He grinned. "The important bits."

Terja smiled, surprised at the humor. His mind swirled with pleasure, desire, and hesitation. Forcing his emotions aside, he turned to kiss Anan as if they were playing childhood games. But their gazes met, and the weaver's eyes held none of the innocence of childhood. Something burned in them that Terja didn't want to recognize. He found himself drawn to Anan—and terrified by the attraction.

His body tensed from the conflicting emotions until Anan slowed and then came to a stop. "We'll go slow. I promise."

He caressed Terja's back and moved with grace and consideration. Slipping lower, Anan leaned close and kissed along his neck, ending with a soft nip on his shoulder. He tucked Terja against his chest, pulling them tight against each other. Terja moaned at the velvety texture that left his skin covered in a sheen of sweat.

A STRONG scent flared through Anan, building his attraction. The waves of pheromones made gentle lovemaking more difficult. Terja's bare skin strengthened the sensual weaving at his touch. He caressed Terja with great care and deliberation. He didn't want anything to break the developing mood as the attraction spun itself between them.

Easing across Terja's chest, he rubbed his thumbs across the nipples. His breath became shallow as a musky smell surrounded them. He pulled away and kissed down Terja's chest while he tried to ignore the hardness trapped between them. With a twist of Terja's nipples, a hiss exploded between his clenched teeth.

He continued to tease as Terja squirmed. "How're you? Do we need to stop?"

"Oh, strands. Don't stop. It's like your fingers are hot coals."

Anan pressed the tip of his tongue along the edge of Terja's ear while continuing to work over the points of flesh between his fingers. He arched against Anan, his body shaking as a loud moan escaped from deep inside.

Hesitant to stop for fear he would break the spell, he stalked the spinner carefully. He trailed his touch down the center of Terja's chest and over his taut stomach. When there was no panic, he slipped his hand over Terja's kilt and cupped his hard cock.

Terja squeezed his eyes closed as a sigh escaped his lips, and he began thrusting. Anan unlaced the bindings and unwound the supple cloth from Terja's slender hips. As the ends of the fabric slipped apart, his hard dick sprung free. The vein-covered length arched up, slapping against his stomach. It hovered there, pulsing in time to the heartbeat Anan could sense where their skin touched. He slid his finger through the thick liquid spinning from the tip of Terja's shaft. The moans increased in volume until he caressed Terja's heaving stomach to give him time to return from the edge of impending orgasm.

Once his breathing returned to something closer to normal, he glided his touch through the thatch of hair surrounding Terja's dripping cock. He grasped it tight, enjoying its length and coarseness. He tugged at the pubic hair surrounding its base, and his reward was a rolling moan.

"Oh, Twined Ones! What's happening?"

Anan nibbled along his neck, careful to not touch his twitching cock. "You're feeling the pleasure of our intimacy. You have pleasured yourself... surely."

"No. Nothing. Like. Oh, Spinner!"

He ran his hand down Terja's torso and grabbed his hard cock again, stroking it once with agonizing slowness. Terja responded with a long groan guaranteed to have all the deathspinners in the valley clicking and scurrying through their webs.

"Ah, strands!"

He tensed and the first stream shot from his cock. The hot thread landed on Anan's arm. The heat and the scent of their sex had him throbbing beneath his kilt. Terja shot again and again. A seemingly unending supply of semen landed on Anan as he held Terja. A few strangled gasps later, he tensed a last time and then collapsed against Anan.

Their matama intertwined as the scent of orgasm surrounded them with such intensity Anan could taste the metallic tang on the back of his tongue. The moment stretched on as they locked eyes, and the finest tendrils of amber flitted through Terja's gaze.

"Better than you thought?" Anan asked.

He could tell Terja struggled to control himself, but the moment made it impossible. He studied Anan with an odd combination of humor and lust. "I've never… done that before. I see why they called it 'little death.' I thought I'd died and became part of the Great Weaving."

"No one?" Anan asked.

"No one?" Terja appeared confused, then lit up with understanding. "I've kissed and touched others. It felt nice, but I didn't know real intimacy was so much more."

"I'm honored to have been your first."

"Yes, but hopefully not my last." He bolted upright and gazed at Anan with desolation etched across his face. "I'm sorry, I wasn't—"

"Kit, calm down. We haven't dishonored anyone. To get the silk, we need to make corcra, to get corcra, we needed to create the intimacy matama by being with each other. If it feels good too, that isn't a bad thing."

Terja started to speak, but his gaze traveled to the fiber they had left beside them. He motioned toward the white filaments, panic on his face. "It didn't work. The matama didn't take."

"Use your sight. What does it look like?"

He snapped his spellspinner sight into place. After a few moments' hesitation, he tried to explain what he saw. "It's still white. But the weaving is moving. The threads are covered with something clear. Like they're waiting for something else." He paused in his description and locked eyes with Anan. "What's missing? Why won't the corcra form?"

Terja's gaze softened for an instant. A swirl of emotions slid over his face too quickly for Anan to interpret. His expression carefully neutral, Terja turned back. "We are only half-finished." He motioned toward the bulge in Anan's kilt.

"No, it has to be something else," Anan said as he recoiled from the act he'd secretly hoped he wouldn't have to perform, in spite of his encouragement of the same thing from Terja.

Terja shook his head slowly. "The threads are seeking something. You must make your half of the gathering. I know of no other way, but I've never done this."

The reality of the situation crashed against Anan, destroying the walls woven since finding his twining dead. He'd performed Silbre's unraveling only days ago. *I should've died at his side.* But he hadn't. First Twining refused him that honor. Now he was left with a naïve spinner who believed spinners and weavers shouldn't form intimate twinings.

Something moved beside him, and he found Terja staring at him. He tightened his jaw and rewove the barriers to the parts of his soul shredded by the past days. He would do his duty to his clan.

"Yes, you're right," Anan said.

Terja spoke into the growing night. "I wish the weavings gave another way for you, too."

"I know." Anan looked down at his failing erection. "I'm afraid it's going to take some effort to get back to where we were."

Terja met his gaze. "How... I don't...."

He realized they had to finish, and Terja needed some guidance. He ran the back of his hand across Terja's cheek.

"Just do what felt good to you, and we'll take it from there."

TERJA LEANED forward, touched Anan's chest, and traced over the beautifully marked patterns that covered him. But the ripples of euphoria traveling up his arms told him the sensation was more than simple pleasure. The feel of thick velvet under his touch coiled through Terja's body, targeting his groin and rapidly recovering cock. Remembering their goal, he struggled to regain his control. He watched the man beside him and considered Anan's suggestion. He studied his muscular form and remembered the fire that roared inside him when his nipples were stroked. He trailed his hands upward, then rubbed over the hard points of flesh on Anan's chest.

Anan sighed and whispered, "Harder."

He took each nipple and pinched down while he rolled them between his thumb and finger.

"Oh strands, yes! That's it."

Emboldened by the response, he worked to duplicate each motion used on him. Soon he unlaced the weaver's kilt. Unable to resist as the lust grew, Terja reach down and squeezed the obvious bulge. He started at the rumbling growl he got in reply.

"That's good. Don't stop."

He hesitated but then unwrapped the kilt from Anan's hips. A masculine scent arose and curled through him. As the kilt fell away, he gripped the rock-hard cock that emerged and squeezed.

Terja pressed lower, caressing and exploring the muscular body in ways that until now happened only in the most secret of his dreams. Fantasies he didn't even admit to himself. He cupped Anan's balls and sent them roiling at this touch.

"It's good. Do whatever you want," Anan said.

He curled his fingers around Anan's shaft and felt the familiar—yet unique—hardness. He pulled the foreskin up until the deep red crown was covered, then slid the skin down to expose it. Fascinated, Terja stroked slowly. Anan groaned again, and he stopped.

"Oh, Twined Ones!"

Terja tightened his grip and began stroking again. This time his fist blurred as it moved up and down Anan's shaft. After a fingercount of strokes, Anan tensed and began to shake. With a soft gasp, the first ribbon of white shot out. In rapid succession more came, the hard shaft jumping with each pulse. Fascinated by the ribbons of translucent white, he smeared the lines that crisscrossed his body. Each bit of cream that landed on Terja seared through his system, creating a net of pure pleasure that cradled him like nothing before. Time stopped as their life strands blended.

Fascinated by the muscles moving and rippling through Anan's hard body, Terja let himself enjoy their moment together.

He's handsome. Why would this be forbidden? Anan glanced up, their eyes met, and the briefest of sparks flared. Then the moment disappeared like a wisp of smoke.

"The silk?" Anan asked.

He scooped up the small cluster of purple threads and held them out to Anan. "All filled."

THE HEAT surrounded Anan as he squatted on the canyon rim, hoping they would complete this task before the sun slept today. As they went through their final plans this morning, they'd discovered a flaw. They needed a living animal to bait their snare. Otherwise the deathspinners would sense them in their colony long before they could escape. So, their day consisted of sitting in the scorching sun to wait for an animal for the webs. They'd come to realize animals didn't stumble into the valley as often as they thought.

As the sun touched the treetops marking the western horizon, two springtails wandered into the area. They demonstrated their naming as they performed jumps that were easily over Anan's head. But they seemed to detect the predators only a few spans away and avoided the fatal webbing. Anan waited, the corcra weaving set and ready to create so he could instantly throw the web over whatever unfortunate animal wandered into the canyon. They needed these two to act as bait, or they lost a day. Anan held his breath with each step the springtails moved closer to the edge of the deathspinner web. Anan hoped he could weave the spell fast enough to keep the animals from escaping.

He tried not to think about it too much. If he missed, they would be another day behind, and the captives would be a day's travel farther away. Anan prepared to pull the corcra from the silk and shoved his doubts away. He gauged the distance and knew the animals were moving out of the range he could throw the netting. It might be pure matama, but it still had the limits of the physical world. In a frenzy, he tried to find a solution.

Anan refocused on the tableau playing out before him as the frontmost springtail bounded farther away, and the web began to grow toward it. The second springtail followed, and Anan knew he couldn't hurl the spell that far.

Terja stepped beside him, sling in hand. He made the barest of motions with his weapon. Anan's brows knotted together; then he realized what Terja was suggesting.

He tripped the spell, and in a fingercount of heartbeats he finished the weaving—and dropped it into the pouch of Terja's sling. In a continuation of the motion, Terja spun his sling and released the spell with a flick of his wrist. The web spread perfectly over the animals. In a few heartbeats, the corcra sank into the springtails, just before the deathspinner's webbing closed around them.

The animals shot upward, trying to escape, but their struggles only wrapped the unbreakable fibers around them more securely. Their struggles became more frantic as the entire colony moved toward them. The creatures clustered over the two small animals, and their struggles stopped. Feeding hordes covered them, and all Anan and Terja could do was watch and wait. The feeding continued as the sun slipped behind the horizon. The animals fed on their prey with terrifying efficiency.

"Look. That one's acting different," Terja said.

Anan followed where he pointed. One of the creatures seemed to be staggering away from the shrouded springtail. While they watched, it slowly sank to the ground. One by one the deathspinners collapsed into unmoving forms.

"They've all stopped moving. Do you think they're asleep?"

"What if there are more inside?"

Anan shrugged. "That would be… unfortunate."

Terja scanned the area, his apprehension clear in the tension of his stance. Anan considered a moment, studying the web closely before pulling his bow from his shoulder and passing it to the spinner.

Terja froze. "Why are you giving me your bow?"

"I'm going in for the eggs. You'll need the bow if something goes wrong. I think I see the pathways in the webbing used by the deathspinners so they don't get entangled in their own web. But if I become trapped…."

"I'm no weaver! The deathspinners are far too small for me to hit with your bow." His expression became thoughtful. "I might be able to give you a little time with my sling."

Anan locked eyes with Terja. "You shoot *me*. If they take me I'm telling you to give me mercy."

Terja examined the bow as if he held a poisonous river serpent. Anan steeled himself, unable to see another choice. By the time their eyes met, he knew this held their best chance for success.

"In the body, the head is too small." He considered Terja for a moment. "Use your sling if you need to, but don't leave me alive."

A shudder traveled through Terja as he replayed Anan's words.

"One of us must rescue the captives, or the Kuri will be a dead clan. We have to succeed, find how they are getting through the village barrier webs, and help any other Talac clans that need it." Anan glanced down the valley. "It's time. The corcra may not keep them asleep very long."

They walked to the outer edge of the webs, and he took a step, followed by another until he was several strides inside the border. Anan froze at some movement but realized the light breeze had sent a loose bit fluttering. Waiting for a moment he breathed a sigh of relief. The web didn't capture him. It appeared that with the deathspinners asleep, the web was quiet.

He skirted the cluster of predators and their prey and watched for a few heartbeats but still saw no movement. His confidence building, Anan sprinted for the densest joining of webs, where they thought the nodules would be.

He reached the man-sized webbings and slipped out his knife. After a glance to each side to check the threads with his spell vision, Anan moved closer. The weave reminded him of a facet of obsidian. He held his knife tight and sent a plea to the Twined Ones, then cut into the gossamer netting.

The stone knife slid through the tough sheets as if they were air. Anan eased the edges of the cut apart and peered inside. The pocket was half-filled with balls of silk. They must be the eggs.

Terja began yelling. Anan turned, more than a little annoyed that he would be so loud.

"Only the small ones! Don't touch the big ones."

Anan peered in and realized there were two sizes. *How could Terja know which to choose?*

TERJA TREMBLED as the weaver sped across the colony grounds, moving closer. Regardless of how fast he ran, he couldn't move fast enough for Terja. He breathed a little easier once Anan passed the feeding area. As he closed the distance to the edge, Terja fought himself to keep from running in to drag Anan to safety. When he crossed the edge of the webbing, Terja grabbed him tight in his arms. Anan's scent wove itself into the air around them, unsteadying Terja for a moment.

"I'm fine," Anan said. "But why just small ones?"

"I remembered something from the teaching tapestries. I didn't understand why, but it said something about large being deadly."

Anan shrugged and made a soft grunt. "Then we'll just take the small ones."

As they placed the eggs in their pack, Terja heard a clicking noise from the webs. The spinners were struggling to their feet. In the next few moments, he discovered he could pack faster than he had thought.

Anan glanced at Terja and then over his shoulder to the gathering deathspinners. He matched Terja's speed as they packed the last few silk eggs away. The rising moons lit the way to their encampment.

What do the nodules have in them? How do you open one? Terja pushed the thoughts aside to focus on their task.

Moonlight provided some illumination to the featureless darkness of the camp. They had a few edible plants Anan had gathered during their journey but little else. Terja brought out the food while the weaver rekindled the fire. He laid their tiny cache of edibles beside the growing blaze.

Terja glanced back to see a woven container about the size of two fists being formed in Anan's hands. As a spellweaver, Anan would be an expert at any type of weaving, but the object taking form far exceeded anything Terja had seen before. But, other than the herdweavers, he had never interacted with anyone other than spinners.

Anan splashed water into the basket and swirled it around. Setting the container to one side, he rolled a few smooth rocks into the fire and then sat on his heels.

Curiosity overcame caution for Terja. "What are you doing?"

Anan jumped, obviously startled out of his thoughts. "Cooking. I can't eat dried kuri and raw groundnuts again."

Terja looked at the basket and the crackling fire. "It'll burn."

"I'm not putting the basket in the fire. My mother taught me how to cook this way."

"Your mother? You never talk about your family."

Anan considered Terja for a moment and then shrugged. "They were killed a year after my spellweaving matured. They were hunting for daggerhorn and were gored. It took us a fingercount of days to find them. I wouldn't have made it through losing them if it hadn't been for him." He turned to look at Terja. "Losing Silbre has been as bad. But this time I will avenge him."

They sat quietly, neither wanting to disturb the thoughts of the other. But a few heartbeats later, Anan turned to Terja. "What about you? You only speak of your father. What about your mother?"

Terja stared into the gathering darkness. "She died when I was young. My father said she went to another clan and was caught in an ambush. I was too young to remember."

Another time of quiet settled over them until Terja spoke again.

"Isiliva."

"What?" Anan asked.

"That was her name. Isiliva."

"What a pretty name. I've never heard it before."

"Father said she was from the Meke clan."

"The Talac mountain people? I've never heard of one of them coming to the flatlands."

Terja started to say something more but reconsidered and settled in to observe Anan cooking. He dumped out the water he'd used to test the basket, put in dried kuri and edible plants, then added water until the container was half-full. Taking two sticks, he carefully lifted one of the hot rocks from the fire and dropped it into the stew.

The rock sizzled and roiled in the water. Once it stopped bubbling, Anan pulled it from the basket and dropped it back into the coals. Then he repeated the process with the other hot rock. Sooner than Terja would have thought, a basket of stew bubbled, and tantalizing smells filled the night air.

Anan fished out the last stone and gave the basket to Terja. He took a sip and smiled. "Good. Much better than dried travel food."

He passed the stew to Anan, who took a careful drink of their meal. "Could use a spice weaving." Anan frowned slightly and took another sip.

Terja grinned, then held out a small wad of fuzz in a multitude of colors. Anan leaned closer, examined the fibers, then looked at Terja.

"It's all ours. Habit."

"No. I'm not complaining. But I didn't think we had any spinner silk left."

"There were bits and pieces. Too short to spin. They couldn't even be used for corcra. Normally a spinner wouldn't bother with fragments so small. But like I've said, I harvest matama from habit. It's just what spinners do. So, I have a pocket full of colorful lint." He motioned toward the tiny pile. "Use what you want. It's all from us."

"Really?"

Terja stopped for a minute and studied Anan. "Who else would it be from?"

Anan's face turned red, and he started to answer when Terja motioned him to silence. "Take what you'd like. I'm as tired of dried kuri as you are."

Anan traced over the careful work and pulled the matama for a simple cooking spell to give their stew some flavor. After a heartbeat or two of weaving, Anan released the spell into their stew.

After sampling the soup again, Anan nodded, and a ghost of a smile came to his lips. "Much better." He held it out to Terja.

He lifted the basket to his lips again and took a sip. His eyes fluttered shut as the pleasant sensations captured in his spinning echoed in his mouth. He knew each spinner and weaver left a unique impression that always flavored the work afterward. It seemed he and Anan formed a rich and flavorful mix that he found satisfying.

He'd been able to distinguish each spinner or weaver's unique signature since he was a kit. His father had delighted in guessing who'd been the cook each night and would loudly voice displeasure if something didn't have its usual flavor.

Terja's brief happiness melted away when his memories returned to the last several days of darkness. Anan seemed to sense his mood change. Their gazes met, and there was a brief mutual exchange of understanding before they refocused on the delicious meal.

They finished the first basket of stew, but both of their stomachs growled.

"I can make more if you'd like," Anan said.

Terja's stomach chose that moment to produce a particularly loud rumble. He smiled shyly at Anan. "I think that was a yes, please."

"It sounded like a yes to me, too."

While Anan cooked the second meal, Terja pulled out one of the spinner eggs to puzzle out how to separate the filaments. His spinning vision revealed little but a mass of unending perfectly smooth threads. There was no beginning or end.

Terja had always been able to unravel anything. Even the most tangled snarls of the Kuri weavers seemed to fall apart at his touch. He leaned closer to the fire for better light. Still trying to see more clearly, he turned again, this time close enough to the cooking basket that steam from their meal curled around the egg. As he scanned the orderly mass of fibers over and over, he noticed his fingers became sticky.

Wait. Sticky? Why would my fingers be sticky? Terja held the egg as close to the steam as he could tolerate, turning it slowly.

"What are you doing?" Anan asked.

"Look." Terja moved his fingers apart, the residue adhering between them.

"What is it?"

"The secret to the eggs is my guess."

Terja slowly turned the fiber sphere, his fingers becoming layered with glue. After studying it closely, Terja stopped rotating the orb and explored the now soft mass. Pulling away slowly, he drew a filament no thicker than the finest hair of Anan's velvet. Drawing the thread out, he fastened it to a convenient twig and then began to unwind.

Terja lost track of time as he unrolled layer after layer of gossamer-fine fiber. The final length unwound into the growing ball. He used the waterskin to rinse the stickiness from his fingers.

"Now we know why we only take the small ones."

Anan appeared confused. "We do?"

"Of course." He held out his empty palm as an answer. Anan studied the vacant hand for a moment before he realized what Terja was demonstrating.

"These aren't eggs at all. They're pure fiber. The big ones must be their egg cases." Anan hissed as the breath shot from him. "If we'd gotten the eggs...."

"We could be dead. If they'd hatched, we would have had hundreds of tiny, lethal deathspinners."

Realization settled over him, and he grinned at Anan. "We did it. We have the silk we need. We've survived so far."

A shy smile slipped across Anan's lips. "We have what we need. You did a great job in translating the weavings. I didn't even know spinners learned the old symbols."

For the first time since the attack, a laugh escaped Terja's lips. "If you ask the old ones enough questions, they will eventually answer you so you will stop bothering them. But I think it's also been a gift from the Twined Ones."

"Well, the stew is cooked, and I'm still hungry. After we're both fed, we can try to unwind another ball of silk."

He raised his hand with hesitation, then placed it on Anan's shoulder and squeezed. The hard muscles sent a ripple of feeling he now recognized through his body. "We've done well."

CHAPTER SEVEN

"WHAT DO you mean you can't find them?" Terja snapped.

"What part don't you understand? The 'can't' or the 'find them'?"

"They must have at least twenty captive Talac with them now, and almost as many Varas. We've been following them for almost a handful of days since the deathspinner colony. You're the great hunter. How can you have lost the path of forty people?"

Anan wanted to drop this insistent annoyance the Firsts burdened him with off a cliff to silence him. What made the situation worse—Terja might be right. Anan began talking, more to himself than anything else. "The trail should be as easy to see as a herd of kuri in shortgrass. But there's nothing, nothing at all. Not a rock turned, not a blade bent, nothing. It's as if a weaver were cleaning up—"

His gaze locked with Terja's, who shook his head in disbelief. "No. It can't be. Surely you're wrong. Another Talac would never— They couldn't—It's too horrible to consider."

"The pass through the hills we saw earlier, the one I said they should use. We're going back there."

"That pass is almost a day behind us. Are you certain?"

"Does your spell sight show you more than mine? Because, unless it does, I don't see other choices." Anger and frustration began to seep past the wall behind which Anan had kept his emotions in check for all this time.

Terja glared until he reached the limit of Anan's tolerance. Anan settled his pack in place and walked down the daggerhorn path they'd been following. This might be another false trail, but at least this time he was aware it might be a deception. Time and patience were in short supply for them both.

He'd only taken a few steps when he heard Terja follow.

The sun was almost to the western horizon by the time they reached the pass. They studied the ground and foliage with spell sight. They couldn't avoid the obvious answer any longer. A spellweaver was working with the Varas and hiding their passage. Neither of them could believe the story unfolding. But as they found clues bit by bit, it became obvious that the unimaginable was fact, a weaver helped the Varas.

"They're helping attack the clans. Why? How? No spinners could be helping. Where is he getting matama from to make his spells?" Anan said. He studied the path again and shook his head. "How could I've missed this? It's so obvious."

Terja gripped his shoulder. "There is no reason to burden yourself. I was wrong to criticize you. No one would ever have considered a Talac helping."

He couldn't meet Terja's gaze. The weaving hiding the slavers' trail took time and skill to find, but once you knew the signs, it was easy to unravel. *How could I have been so stupid? I should never have missed this.* He settled his carrying bag into place and adjusted his quiver and bow. Anan studied the steep foothills ahead of them. They would find these slavers, and if any survived they could tell any other Varas the cost of being in Talac lands.

TERJA'D FOLLOWED Anan since they'd discovered the hidden trail, and now the disc of the sun sunk behind the horizon. As he considered the man in front of him, he realized his opinions of the large weaver were a tangle no spinner could separate. But in the midst of everything, he'd come to enjoy Anan's touch. The soft velvet and hard muscles became a needed refuge each night. After pleasuring each other and collecting the corcra needed to get the deathspinner eggs, they'd begun sharing a bed at night. More companionship than anything more, but he'd come to relish waking each morning with Anan next to him.

His mind struggled to reconcile the teachings of a lifetime saying weavers were of a lower station. He might not always agree with the big weaver, but he'd come to understand he was no better than Anan. What he'd been taught as undeniable facts didn't hold up under close examination. In fact, he'd come to realize most of his prejudices had come from one or two spinners, mostly his father.

Terja adjusted his pack basket and trotted to catch up. The weaver set a ground-eating pace that left Terja with little desire for conversation. They traveled in silence until the sun dipped below the western horizon.

"This is their trail. They can't be moving fast with the number of slaves they have. From the signs, they're chained to each other. We should catch up in a few days. But if they're taking the time to hide their trail, they think someone might be following them. We'll need to watch for traps that might be on their backtrail."

He took a deep breath and fixed his gaze on Terja. "I'm tired of dried kuri, even in stew. Springtail tracks are thick. I think we should try to hunt before darkness settles around us."

Terja's stomach growled at the thought of fresh meat. "I agree. Roasted springtail is our goal for tonight."

"Good. This may be the last time we can risk a fire. I'd like one night of rest on a full stomach."

Terja pulled a small pouch from his pack and opened it. The container was his spinner's case, and inside were several packets of white silk, along with several hanks of silk already filled with matama. He saw the surprise on Anan's face as he studied the work.

"I harvested a little each night. But this should be enough to make the guardian web so we don't need to build a thorn barrier tonight. That will give us more time to hunt."

Anan smiled, lowered his pack to the ground, and pulled his bow from across his shoulders. "I saw daggerhorn tracks a short distance back too. Roasted daggerhorn would be so good." *And I can do the sweetgrass burning for Silbre. It's time to fulfill my obligation.*

69

Terja pulled his sling from around his waist and smiled at Anan. "I'll focus on the springtail, then. Care to see who returns with game first? Perhaps they can clean the take."

Anan turned and started down the hill at a sprint. "You're on, little spinner."

ANAN GLANCED back over his shoulder to make certain he was out of sight of their camp. Not a day passed that he didn't mourn the loss of his mate. The burden was beginning to affect his weaving, to the point he was missing important details like he had today. He knew it was time to unweave the pain he'd been walling away since the day he felt their bond snap.

He pulled the tight braid of sweetgrass from his kilt and searched for a spot to perform the release. After a few moments he saw a group of three ironwood trees that formed a perfect triad. He cleared the area, created a small hearth of flat rock in the middle, and laid the braid in its center. He wasn't certain how this weaving was performed, but he knew they wouldn't survive if he didn't.

"Silbre, I'm not sure what to say to you. Our bond was tight, and you were my rock when things were hard. Now…. Now I guess I'm the rock and half of the only chance of saving the Talac who were taken. It's been difficult. Very difficult. But the spinner I must work with is learning."

He studied the sweetgrass, but there was no sign that anything was happening. "Why should I be surprised it wasn't that easy? I have to say the things I don't want to say out loud."

The walls inside Anan began to crumble, freeing the emotions inside him. The darkness filled his mind as tears began to roll down his cheeks like a rivulet filled with spring floods. A sob wretched itself free as the pain seared through his system.

"Silbre. You will always be a part of me. I will celebrate our time together every day, but my feelings for Terja are growing with each challenge we face together. I fought it. I swear to you. But it's as strong as our bond was. I am drawn closer to him each day."

Another wave of grief passed through Anan, punctuated by a sob that shook his being.

Unable to think, Anan dropped his head and cried quietly. His tears ran down his face and dripped onto the sweetgrass he had left. He ignored everything at first, but when his pain lessened, he noticed the sweetgrass was darkening to a deep red.

The braid suddenly transformed into a small cloud that lifted into the sky. It elongated into the shape of a bird. The wingtips swung in to touch Anan's cheeks. The pain lessened at the caress, and the shape disappeared like a wisp of smoke.

Anan blinked, and the world shifted back. But the intricate braid was gone, and Anan felt a peace that had escaped him since the attack.

He stood and backed away. After staring vacantly for a moment, Anan scanned the ground around him. There was a fresh daggerhorn track with its split-hoof clearly marking its path.

"I guess you're telling me to get busy, Silbre." Anan smiled at the distant sound of a predatory bird claiming its territory.

TERJA HEARD soft footsteps drifting through the gathering dusk. He moved away from the fire, until he made out Anan's silhouette against the fading sky. Relief flooded him at the sight of the weaver. His feelings might be mixed, but he didn't think he could recover if something were to happen to Anan now. He moved toward the fire, and as Anan stepped into the light, he could see the young daggerhorn over his shoulder.

Anan smiled as he glanced at the pair of springtail Terja had already begun to roast on a spit over the coals. "It looks like both of us were successful. And I'm hungry enough to fight a longtooth for either of those springtail!"

"You might have to fight me, then. But they're ready."

Anan hung his take from a nearby tree and took the roasted meat he was handed. The springtail leg was almost as big as his fist, and when he bit into the cooked flesh, juices coated the velvet around his mouth, a small dribble running down his chin. He rolled his eyes and moaned softly. "Oh, Terja. They're perfect. After all the days of dried kuri, my tongue thanks you."

Terja pulled the other springtail from the fire, pried off the meaty leg, and sank his teeth into the crisp outer flesh. The hot juices were soon streaming down his face too. As he bit off another piece, his stomach growled in anticipation.

Terja patted his midsection. "Easy. Let me chew it first."

Anan sucked the last of the meat from the bone, his eyes dancing. "You better feed him. He might be dangerous."

Terja pulled off another leg and gnawed at the meat. Talking stopped as both men lost themselves in the first real meal they'd eaten since this nightmare began. Terja enjoyed a sensation of peace he refused to question. He knew the reprieve would be short-lived. But his layers of biases against weavers were unraveling. The more time he spent with Anan, the more he respected the big weaver and the more he worried about something happening to him.

Anan cracked a bone open to suck out the marrow before tossing the remains into the coals. He licked each finger before gazing at Terja. "This is the first time in a long while that my belly has been happy."

Terja grinned as he tossed the remains of his meal into the fire with Anan's. "That was good. The springtails were young and tender."

Anan glanced over his shoulder and motioned at the daggerhorn. "We'll need to dry the meat. If we cut it thin we can take it in the morning."

He glanced around, seemingly ill at ease as he unconsciously wiped his hands on his bare chest. Terja found himself wanting to curl against the thick velvet there.

Both men seemed lost in their thoughts as they prepared for the night. Anan wove the guardian web around them, using the threads Terja had harvested since they'd gotten fresh silk. With the fire banked, they lay next to each other for warmth against the growing night chill.

Terja moved close, his arms tucked against his sides rather than draped across Anan as he would like. He pressed his bare chest against the velvet of his back and gasped.

"Something wrong?"

Terja pressed his lips together to keep another moan from escaping. Once the sensation passed, he relaxed slightly. "No. No problem." He hesitated for a moment before continuing. "Your warmth is nice."

Anan turned until their gazes met, and held the connection until Terja looked away. Without a word, he covered them with one of the kuri weavings they'd found. His arms wrapped around Terja and pulled them tight against each other.

The blanket trapped the warmth of their bodies, and Terja drifted toward sleep. A shiver washed over him when Anan tilted his head and kissed his cheek.

"Pleasant dreams."

"You too."

For the first night since the attack, Terja slept without being awakened by night terrors.

Chapter Eight

Geir paced to the front of the caravan, slaves scurrying to stay out of his path. *I swear to the Burning Twins, if this is another stunt from Kotu I will cut him open and leave him for one of those vicious packs of animals that cover this godsforsaken place.* He pushed his way to the head of their caravan, to find Kotu standing and looking at the path in front of them.

"Why are we stopped?" Geir snapped.

"Because of that." Kotu pointed ahead of them.

At first glance Geir thought they'd found another bizarre type of tree. But when he studied the valley, he saw a forest covered in white webbing. It filled the small valley they intended to travel. "What is it?"

Kotu shrugged, then showed a feral smile that highlighted his sharpened teeth. There were stories whispered of Kotu ripping out his victim's throat with those teeth. But Geir had dealt with men of Kotu's ilk before. He would never trust his second, ever. Geir gained some comfort in the fact that he alone knew all the pass phrases, bribes, and gifts needed to travel from these lands to the blessed river.

"We don't know. When the slaves spotted it, they wouldn't go any closer. Not even using the whips on them."

Bloody stripes covering the tall bodies around him attested to their efforts. If this continued most of the slaves wouldn't be fit for the pleasure pits, if they survived at all. But they couldn't let the slaves dictate their choices.

"Get Xain."

Kotu scowled but motioned for someone to find the traitor. His glare remained as he locked gazes with Geir. *Is today when he leaves me no choice but to kill him?* But he broke the gaze to stare at the ground before forcing Geir into action. A moment later the men returned with Xain walking between them.

"What do you need, Captain?"

Geir pointed to the web-encased trees. "What is that, and why are the slaves so frightened?"

Xain's gaze locked on the scene before him. Geir was surprised when he gasped and dropped back a step.

"Deathspinners...."

"Oh, flaming twins! Explain, you superstitious animal," Geir said.

"They're living death. Of a horrible kind. They're also the source of the fiber for storing Talac spells, but only the twice-damned spinners know the secret of getting the silk."

Kotu erupted into a harsh laugh. "Another superstition. It's a big crawler. No different than the ones we have along the river."

"Deathspinners are nothing like anything along your river. Of that I can guarantee you."

Kotu glanced at the huddled slaves and pointed to one taken at the final village they'd attacked. "You, come here."

The young man rose jerkily, as if someone else controlled his arms and legs. He froze, unwilling to move. A slaver jabbed his spear tip into the Talac. With a gasp he stepped forward as the blood flowed down his back. A few steps put him within Kotu's reach.

Geir knew what Kotu planned but didn't intercede when he shoved the man forward. "Walk to the first tree and return, and you'll live today."

The Talac stared down the ravine as if seeing the sight for the first time. He suddenly turned on the Varas with the ferocity of a trapped animal. He fought his way past the surprised guards and almost succeeded in escaping. At the last instant, Kotu's whip circled his throat and yanked him backward. The whip came alive in Kotu's hand, peeling layers of skin from the Talac.

The Talac's fear of the deathspinners far exceeded any punishment. He fought savagely, breaking Kotu's nose, whose face contorted with insane fury as blood gushed. He made a hideous noise, then rammed his forearm-long knife into the Talac's gut and yanked sideways. With anger-fueled strength, he grabbed the fatally wounded man by the arm and threw him down the hillside. The Talac slave erupted into screams of terror.

A knot of people watched, but before Kotu could voice disdain, the webbing rippled and trapped the Talac. The man screamed again and again until webbing sealed his mouth... and the deathspinners came. Geir attempted to catalog the animals scurrying from the trees in hordes. His heart hammered at the sight. Xain was right. These were nothing like the crawlers occasionally found along the great river. As the colony's leading edge reached the weakly struggling man, his body locked. But his eyes bulged in his skull, and his mouth opened in a silent scream.

Xain grabbed a crossbow from a guard, snapped the butt against his shoulder, and released the quarrel. The wood and iron buried itself between the victim's eyes, who submerged a heartbeat later under a seething mass of bodies. Xain slammed the crossbow into its owner's hand. He wove his way through the crowd to stop in front of Geir.

"The deathspinner venom keeps its victim alive for as long as a moon while they feed on the dissolving body. The Talac would not condemn even you to them." He sneered at Kotu. "You, they'd make an exception for."

Xain motioned toward the captives. "None of them will go down the valley. They know what a deathspinner is, and they'd all rather you beat them to death. It would be less painful."

He waited for a few moments, then returned to the caravan. Geir gathered himself, knowing even his most hardened men were shaken by what they'd witnessed—except Kotu.

Their eyes met, and the fever burned in Kotu's hungry gaze. Geir recoiled at the lack of mercy in those eyes. The deathspinners would be too gentle a death for Kotu.

"No," Geir said.

"Captain, I have not asked a boon of you."

"You threw your toy to those creatures. Find your satisfaction somewhere other than the captives."

Kotu glared and swiped the blood from his face, flinging the crimson drops at the huddled slaves. His black glance dared them to give him a reason to unleash his anger, and hunger, on another Talac. When none did, he stomped through the slavers surrounding him, knocking them out of his way.

Geir waited until Kotu disappeared from sight, then motioned to one of his sergeants. "We're backtracking until we find a location for an extended encampment. Prepare the men."

The man barked out orders. Soon the caravan reversed its direction. They'd pushed hard to reach Varas lands, and further delays were unacceptable. The fear existed that Geir might fail his backer, and if that happened the deathspinners would be a preferable fate. These were not people to be trifled with. He knew the dark rumors that some House of the Sun members enjoyed Talac pelts for bedding.

He stared into the distance, hopeful still that his real goal would be met. Money was nothing when your family was dying slowly around you. He would find a peltless Talac to save his children. When he'd left, several were showing the first symptoms of the wasting disease that had already taken his oldest son. The ruin readers had assured him the cure was with the Talac. He would be the first Varas to take one of the peltless ones alive and save the last of his family.

Geir spun on his heel, walking a few steps behind the last guard. The whips cracked above the Talac as the handlers turned them. Today had to be the last of the leniency for Xain. He had touched a Varas without permission, a forbidden act. Granted, the slave wasn't long for this world; he couldn't allow Xain to return to the great river alive. He was saddened at the necessity. The traitor had proven more useful than he expected. Geir had saved him from the pits on a hope he would prove useful in defeating the Talac magic and in finding a peltless Talac. But he'd soon discovered Xain was valuable in ways Geir had not expected. He could fill the need Geir's addiction fueled.

They would leave this Twins-forsaken country for the soft green surrounding the Varas homelands. Once they were deep in Varas territory, he would give Xain to Kotu. With any luck, they'd kill each other.

With a sigh, he moved toward his own tent.

JOVEN SAT shivering while Morea leaned against him. Tremors filled both of them, but not from any summer chill. That day's death could have been one of them. Morea's feet showed no improvement. Joven still carried her, and when that was added to the constant barrage of fresh whip marks, Joven faded each day. Today he had realized why a bit of matama was lost from his kilt. Somehow Xain stole matama from them. The traitor didn't need permission to pull the energies into his own weavings. With Joven's own vision as weak as a kit's, he couldn't weave any better than a weak novice. This sense of helplessness was new to Joven. His spell sight had been strong since his adult velvet grew in.

He distantly registered the tableau playing out between Geir, Kotu, and Xain. After the horror of a fellow Talac being thrown to the deathspinners, most of the slaves focused on being unnoticed. Everyone braced themselves for what would come next.

When Xain grabbed the crossbow and gave the Talac mercy, Joven had been shocked. It took bravery to end the Talac's suffering. But he'd also been responsible for wiping out several Talac clans. Given his slight mercy today, he would at least offer the traitor a quick death.

Joven prepared himself when the whips cracked, expecting their bite. But to his surprise, no lightning strikes of leather added to the dense web of half-closed injuries covering his body. Stifled grunts of pain whispered up and down the line of captives as they struggled to their feet. Joven wasn't surprised when they reversed their march. Even the soulless Varas could understand the impossibility of moving through a deathspinner colony. Kotu's demonstration had left little doubt.

He knelt to allow Morea onto his back. He braced himself for the pain of her slight weight against his raw skin, but instead of the familiar clambering of his friend, Morea slipped her hand in his. "I can walk. They can't move us far before dark. They'll want everyone chained in place before then."

Joven stared at her, his fog-shrouded mind trying to make sense of her words. When enough time passed for the mists of exhaustion to lighten, her insight slipped through. With Morea's encouragement, he joined the shuffling mass of Talac. Even the newest captives hung their heads and stared at the ground. As they moved closer to the eastern border of Talac territory, hope faded for everyone.

Thank the Twined Ones, the trip ended quickly. The encampment chosen would be comfortable for several days, with luck even a bit longer. They'd traveled at a fast pace for close to half a moon now, and many captives had reached the limits of their endurance. They were herded toward an open area where they dropped to the ground. A few guards watched over them while the other Varas made camp. Joven wrapped his arms around his legs where he sat, unable to move or care. A few days of rest gave the only hope for Morea's feet to heal. The pause also provided Joven the chance of living another handful of days.

IT HAD been a few days since they left the horrible colony of those lethal animals. But now Geir was more concerned about another animal he had to deal with. The Talac in front of Geir carried a latticework of half-healed lacerations and oozing infection. Geir struggled to contain his anger at the damage, and while no one would answer his questions directly, he knew what happened. This slave had drawn Kotu's attention. And he'd hoped by damaging the pelt, the Talac would be rejected from the auction block. The House of the Sun wanted their slaves in perfect condition. He had mutilated this one in the hope Geir would give the slave to him, and he could satisfy his appetites.

Kotu was wrong.

"This slave is damaged past what the auction block will tolerate. How did this happen?" Geir said. "In this condition he's worth nothing. Does no one recognize the money we're losing?"

Xain squatted beside Joven and prodded at the wounds, his face a mask of distaste when a few of the more severe wept on him. He wiped his fingers on the ground and then stood. "Geir, you know what happened to this boy—and why."

"Take care at your words, Talac."

He lowered his head in respectful obedience. "Yes, Geir, of course. But this slave is too damaged for the auction block."

"Can you repair the damage enough to make him salable?"

Xain examined the network of injuries and flinched. "Perhaps, but he'll be unfit for anything other than the pits."

"Do it. At least the sex pits are some coin in my purse."

"Captain."

"Yes."

"I could also leave a surprise for any Talac that might try to heal him. In case anyone might try to rescue him. It wouldn't affect his worth in the pits."

Geir studied Xain for a few moments, then nodded. "Do it."

Xain grabbed Joven's chin and pulled him so their eyes locked. He seemed unable to break their gaze until Xain touched the panel on Joven's kilt. The final threads of matama faded from the filthy cloth as he hovered over the gashes crisscrossing Joven's torso. Some injuries closed while others stayed unchanged. As he moved back and forth, Joven clenched his teeth.

By the time he stopped, he'd left Joven on his hands and knees, gasping. Geir watched the slave twist in pain, knowing it was due to the special magic being added.

Geir shook his head. *I hope some of them live. Otherwise, I've sold myself to the Burning Twins for no good reason. And worse, my family is lost.*

"JOVEN? JOVEN!"

His eyes focused on the oval face in front of him. He smiled, thinking for a minute they had returned to the savanna and he'd fallen asleep while playing with Morea and her little brother.

"Morea."

"Oh, thank the Twined Ones. You're alive. They brought you back and dumped you. I was afraid you were going to die."

Joven awoke from his hallucination and started to stand, but Morea stopped him. "No, wait. Let me get you some water."

She scrambled away to return a moment later, held a waterskin, and poured liquid over his face and into his half-opened mouth. With his first swallow his system filled with cool, fresh water. Not at all what he expected. Taking the skin, he drank deeply and enjoyed the taste as if it were a sweet.

Once he finished, he handed the nearly empty container to Morea. She still studied him with a worried expression. He patted her arm, feeling better than in recent memory. "Relax, Morea. The traitor's weaving worked. I'm stronger, and the pain's gone."

"Joven. He wasn't… skilled."

Joven rolled his shoulder, tension moving in a wave across the network of new scars. A webwork of pink welts the width of his smallest finger covered his chest. The discussion of the Varas pits filled his mind. "How bad?"

Morea began to speak several times, and then with a sigh she shook her head. "Worse than your chest."

Joven shrugged, the fight beaten out of him. "I don't want to live to get to the Varas homelands. I won't spend the last few days or moons of my life as a toy for men like Kotu."

A tear rolled down Morea's cheek. But Joven couldn't comfort her; he'd already shed his own tears. He couldn't let his emotions escape the container where he'd shoved them. He glanced at Xain when the traitor walked past. Joven wondered if he'd done him a favor by healing him. His talents were obviously limited. The best

Talac spellweavers could have closed the gashes and left an almost invisible mark, but now he was scarred beyond redemption.

Xain glanced toward him, and their eyes locked. Their gaze continued until a fitful breeze slipped into the glade, and they looked away from each other. Xain dropped his gaze to the ground and, with an almost imperceptible shrug, disappeared deeper into the maze of tents.

Joven glanced around to find Morea staring at him. A smile flickered across his lips, and he tousled her hair. "I have no idea what that was about. None."

Morea flicked up the edge of her mouth for Joven and then lifted her foot to examine the soles. Joven traced his finger over her raw feet, and shock ran through his body. He could sense the threads of her injuries. He reached out carefully, using the last thread of healing from Morea's kilt, then settled back. His vision clearly showed him what he needed to know about her injuries as if it had never weakened. He froze, hoping no Varas spotted his reaction. Trying not to draw attention to himself, he checked the matama of the Varas. Their weave differed tremendously from the Talac. *Are all Varas the same?* Their captors' matama were unbalanced webs barely recognizable as people.

A slaver turned to Joven, and he let the sight drop. Even those few moments of vision and releasing the threads of healing on Morea's feet exhausted him. He settled against her wearing a grim smile. His revived spellweaving wouldn't be enough to save him, not when his panels were empty. But the return of his sight gave him hope, however slight it might be. Regardless, he wasn't going to the Varas homeland to be a sex slave until some perversion worse than Kotu bought his life for some act too horrid to imagine. He'd make certain that never happened.

CHAPTER NINE

"CAPTAIN! CAPTAIN. The scouts reported a sun-touched Talac."

Geir locked the messenger in his gaze. He considered for a moment. Only a few days remained before they reached the edge of the Varas lands. But a sun-touched....

"They're certain? This isn't a mistake? How large of a group does it travel with?"

"He was very certain, sir. The sun-touched is only with a few others. Maybe a family group of the animals."

He nodded. A sun-touched pleasure slave would bring an incredible price. They were in high demand by the members of the House of the Sun, but one had not been taken in his lifetime. He knew the High Regency would buy the slave. If he could deliver the legendary golden Talac, he would never need to venture on the grasslands again. But he must be taken alive and undamaged.

"Find Kotu. Send him to me." He turned with a grim look to the messenger. "Tell him there will be toys he can break." The messenger's face went white, and he sprinted into the encampment.

He had barely started planning when Kotu arrived. Their gazes met, and Geir saw the hunger that made this man enjoy his work so much. "The scouts found a sun-touched. I want that Talac. Alive and undamaged."

Unholy glee played across his lieutenant's features. "And the others?"

He swallowed hard as haunting guilt filled him as it did each time he released the restraints and sent this butcher on a mission. He pitied the survivors. He'd seen the results of Kotu's attention before, and they disgusted him. But he was effective. "The others are yours.

I don't want to know what you do to them." Geir took a deep breath. "None of them need to be brought back."

Kotu's lips contorted into a smile that sent a chill through him.

SONERI TOSSED the ball to Dieta and smiled at her nonsense words. It didn't matter that he couldn't understand the kit. He'd been given the task of caring for his youngest sister while their mother and aunt prepared the evening meal. Suddenly a twang of discord slammed into him. The guard web was down!

"Varas! Varas!" He snatched up the child just as a bolt slammed into his mother and she pitched forward, dying. He grabbed for his longbow and spun, managing to launch an arrow into one of the Varas before the first weighted net slammed into him. Clasping the baby to his chest, he struggled against the net, slashing a hole as the warrior glass of his knife sliced through the fiber like mist.

Another net twirled around his legs, and as he lost his footing he heard the scream of his brother from the edge of their small camp. The baby hampered his ability to fight, but he would protect her with his last breath.

More Varas came at him, pummeling him with thick staffs until one particularly vicious strike hit his shoulder, and the baby slipped from his numb hands. "Twined Ones! No!"

He fought the Varas with more ferocity than a trapped daggertooth. His knife bit into more than one of the attackers as he struggled to protect his sister. He snarled and jumped, but thick staff butts connected with the base of his skull, and his world went black.

He jerked awake in an unfamiliar camp, yanked his hands, and felt cold iron bite into his wrists. Struggling ferociously, he discovered he'd been shackled wrists, ankles, and neck. He could barely move, and his hands were attached to a chain running around his waist. No way to fight. Any chance at freedom… gone. A Varas with a smirk stood in front of him.

"Welcome, sun-touched. I am Kotu, the one who organized this tribute to the Red Gods. And to think I thought you were only a legend of old women. Now I understand Geir's excitement."

Soneri spat in his face.

Kotu grabbed him and closed his fingers over his throat, cutting off his air. Time lost all meaning as his vision darkened and he struggled to breathe. He slipped into unconsciousness.

Soneri awoke with a gasp, and a leering face in front of him, a scant handspan from his face. "I was ordered to bring you back. That's the only reason you're alive while the others died. Although they were pleasurable while they lasted."

The agony of Kotu's words ripped through him, and Soneri lunged and tried to bite the Varas. Startled, he stumbled backward, landing in a heap. A ripple of laughter traveled through the crowd of Varas, and his tormentor's face turned scarlet. He motioned to four of the men surrounding them. "Secure him in my tent. Remember, no marks."

The Varas grabbed him, and Soneri fought like a wild animal. But the shackles did their job, and soon one of the men ground his face into the packed dirt while others held his legs. The ugly one dusting off his pants made Soneri fight harder. The brute holding his head pulled out his long knife, and he begged the Twined Ones for release. But the Varas reversed his knife and brought the pommel down on the back of Soneri's head. His vision swam with points of light, and he lost control over his arms and legs. They moved him into the tent as if he were a kuri to the knife.

They did their work quickly and left him chained to poles imbedded in the ground, arms and legs spread wide. Kotu entered the tent, leaving the flap blowing in the breeze. He walked to him and drew his knife across Soneri's nipple. The point of flesh bled freely, leaving a trail of red down his stomach and chest. He repeated the act on the other side, and soon his golden velvet was streaked with red.

The knife flicked out again, this time cutting the laces of Soneri's kilt. It uncurled from around his body and fell to the ground. He studied Soneri with an intensity that chilled his heart. "Nice. Older than I prefer. But I'm certain you will perform well."

The Varas opened his pants, let them drop to his ankles, and stepped out of the pile of fabric. Soneri spent the rest of the night learning the ways someone could be damaged without it showing.

CHAPTER TEN

ANAN WATCHED the Varas camp from the dense coverage of guardian brush. In the last day, they'd discovered the captives. Each movement he made was with exaggerated care as he worked past the finger-length thorns in order to study the encampment. The kilts were replenished, and their chance of accomplishing their task increased. He glanced at the lithe spinner and realized, not for the first time, while Silbre had been amazing, Terja had some equally strong traits himself. He had shown his bravery the numerous times he'd stood at Anan's side. He was discovering the spinner was far more than a spoiled kit. Anan motioned the figure closer and pointed toward the gap in the branches.

Terja moved beside Anan, careful to avoid the fatal thorns. He studied the scene while Anan waited, giving the spinner enough time to find any details he might have missed. Terja turned and motioned him back the way they'd come. The two of them worked their way out of the thicket, creeping away until their whispered information would not be overheard.

Terja vibrated with nervous excitement. "It's them. We found them."

"Yes, I recognized a few people from our clan, but others I've never seen. Some of the clothing is Pero, but other clans are mixed in too."

"How are we going to rescue them?"

"This is a larger raiding party than we thought—several fingercount of Varas. They also have some way to break the protective webbing of spellweavers who were much more experienced than I am."

Terja tensed, let out his breath in a stream that hissed through his teeth. "We can't let the Varas escape, and we have to free the captives."

"I know. But if we attack directly, they'll kill the Talac. A rash decision could get one or both of us killed, too. I have no intentions of failing the bloodweaving we swore."

Terja appeared thoughtful as he considered Anan's words. "We have to decrease their numbers. But the deaths have to appear accidental."

"Exactly. We need a plan." Anan paused, then continued. "They appear to be making preparations to stay here for a few days. We need to find a safe place, one the Varas won't be able to find. From there we can eliminate any of them who get careless until we find a way to free the captives. Whatever caused them to stop is on our side."

Terja thought for a moment, then nodded in agreement. "Once they leave the foothills they are in Varas lands, and we will not be able to reach them."

Anan walked back the direction they came from. He remembered a particular place that drew his attention. "This should work."

Terja searched for shelter and found nothing. "What should work?"

"The cave."

Terja carefully studied the valley around them, first up one side and then repeating his scrutiny on the other. Unable to locate any type of opening, he admitted defeat. "What cave?"

If Terja can't find the entrance, I don't think a Varas from the Great River will either. He stepped close to where the valley wall showed a slight bulge, pulled aside the branches of the featherleaf tree, and exposed a gaping black hole. Terja looked at him in surprise. "How in the ravelings did you find this?"

He pointed to the small spring the width of Terja's hand that made its way under the trees to continue down the hillside. "Water below." He motioned to the dry bank higher up the hillside. "No water above...."

Terja shook his head but made his way through the trees serving as a gateway. Anan followed close behind and let the limbs spring together behind them. They ducked to enter, but the cave stretched for several body lengths. The stream ran along one wall to form a small pool at its lip. Opposite the crystal clear water ran a rock ledge spanning its depth.

There were signs of recent inhabitants but nothing large enough to cause concern. The shelter would be too small for a longtooth pack. They favored dens on the open grasslands anyway. That allowed them to see any interlopers long before they moved close.

Terja surveyed the cave. "This will work. The Varas could walk past and never know we're here. So long as we're careful, they will not find us."

Anan laid his carrying bag on the rock shelf and pulled his longbow from his shoulder. He checked every detail of his equipment before meeting Terja's gaze. "We need meat. I saw daggerhorn tracks not far from here."

"I'll clean out the cave and make sure there are no crawlers that might make our stay unpleasant."

Without another word, Anan disappeared into the dense foliage.

THEIR PERFECT camp discovered, they worked to gather more food while they had time. After leaving early that morning, Anan stalked a daggerhorn for some time and readied himself as it walked closer. He nocked his arrow as he waited for the buck to take the last steps to bring him into the perfect position. But it froze, glanced to the opposite side of the rise, and bounded from sight. He sighed in frustration and moved to see what startled the animal.

He crept closer in the hope he could still take the buck. But he knew there wasn't much chance of that.

Anan froze. *Voices?*

He dropped behind cover as the sounds increased in volume. Raising his head slightly, he saw a slaver driving a Talac ahead of him. He recognized the young man as one of the herdweavers but couldn't recall his name.

A strangled cry came from the Talac as he pitched headlong onto the ground. Anan worked frantically to come up with a plan to save the youngster without sacrificing everything and everyone else.

THE VARAS'S rough hand held Joven immobile as he stared blankly around the opening in the forest, all hope of survival drained from him. Hirvio was one of the cruelest of the slavers, almost as soulless as Kotu. "Well, Talac. Kotu said you're so damaged I don't even need to bring back a pelt for his stash. Although I may save yours for myself. It's been so long since I haven't had to worry about damaging one of you."

Joven fell on his face, too exhausted to move. Hirvio kicked him in the ribs. "Get up. It's time for me to have what I want. Feel free to scream too. I made sure we were far enough away that no one will hear you. Actually, make sure you scream. It's better."

The slaver looped a length of leather around his throat as Joven crawled to his hands and knees. The cord around his neck tightened, cutting off his breath for a heartbeat. He closed his eyes, fighting the panic his own death brought. He couldn't help but wonder, *just strangled?* After the horrors he'd experienced over the days since his capture, strangling would be a kind end.

In spite of his hope to die quietly, he fought for breath as the thong cut off life-giving air. He gasped as the strap loosened, panting hard. A shudder traveled through him when Hirvio ran the tips of his fingers through his velvet. He cried out as the iron of Hirvio's knife cut along his forehead for a finger length. Blood streamed down his face, the sting of the cut adding another layer to his pain.

Hirvio ran his finger across the sheet of crimson, then licked it from his finger. "I think I will take your pelt for myself. I wonder how long I can keep you alive while I flay you. But I need relief first."

The leash tightened again, closing his mind to the horror of Hirvio's plans. He groped at his swollen crotch as he stared at Joven. There was no doubt the Varas enjoyed the idea of torture. Horror left him unable to move when Hirvio opened the lacing on his pants, pulled his hard cock out, and slapped him with it.

"We'll see how good you are. Maybe I'll kill you before I take your pelt if you please me. Maybe."

He took a step closer, the stench attacking Joven's senses, almost making him care if he lived. He knew the appetites of many of the slavers. There were screams from the tents every night as Talac were introduced to Varas desires.

There was a splatter across him, and the garret cinched tight, cutting off all air. *This is it. Now I die.* He looked up, and his world shifted.

THE VARAS folded and collapsed across his kneeling captive. From the time Anan had spotted the two, he knew this would be their first rescue. He hoped to accomplish it without losing their advantage of surprise.

He worked closer as quickly as possible. He'd almost taken a shot when the Varas sliced into the boy's head and described skinning him alive. These people were abominations. He knew he couldn't let the Varas find out about him and Terja. They needed secrecy.

For some, the boy would have been an acceptable loss to keep their secret. For Anan, acceptable losses didn't exist.

He moved faster, seeing the man open his pants. He had to take his shot; this couldn't go further.

Anan drew his bow. After pausing for a heartbeat, he focused on the rapist's head. The arrow released with the hiss of air through the fletching to pierce the man an instant later.

He sprinted toward them, bow in one hand, club in the other. The already dead Varas tensed, tightening the loop around the boy's throat, and fell to the ground. Anan swung his warrior sword, and the leather parted like kuri cheese. The slaver hadn't collapsed before he'd ripped the leather from the boy's throat and hurled it into the brush. He caught the Talac as he fell forward.

"Peace. We're here to help."

Two eyes opened in the blood-coated face, and then he blinked. "Am I dead?"

Anan smiled. "No. You're alive." He hesitated for a moment, seeing the crisscross of scars on the young man. "I can stop the bleeding. If you'll bear my touch." The gaze leveled was one of indifference. He reached for the matama from his spell panels.

He touched the youngster's head and wove the flesh together, working quickly but carefully—Anan didn't want to add another scar to the already laced skin. The cut sealed shut as he sent the last of the weaving along the wound to flush out any poison that might remain.

Anan used his sight to scan the horrifying network of festering wounds that covered this young one. The wounds had been sealed, but not purged. If there were only a few, the boy might survive. But with this many....

He began healing the worst, knowing if he didn't the youngster might die before he got him back to their shelter. In some the wound fever pooled just under the surface, but the most dangerous collected in his organs. He layered threads of green and blue over infection in islands of red and orange. His weaving cooled the fevered wounds, but he realized healing this youngling required more time than he could take in the middle of an open glade. But he needed help. All traces of the three of them must be erased from the site so the Varas wouldn't know they'd been there.

Anan cleaned the worst of the damage to the boy, glad to see the purple welts shrink and cool to pink. The young man's expression was a void. When Anan pulled him up, he moved without resistance. He knew the boy's mind was fragile, but they had little time.

"Name?"

His head tilted slowly, and he considered Anan for a moment. Then with a voice that sounded like he'd been swallowing live coals, he said, "Joven. I'm Joven."

"All right, Joven. We have to move the body. We have to find some place to hide it."

The young man studied him for a few moments. "I have an idea."

TERJA LISTENED for a moment and heard nothing more than the soft twitter of birds in the surrounding trees. Taking that as a sign he was alone, he untied his kilt and let it slip to either side. He ran his hand over himself, cupping his balls and tugging at them. The gentle exploration caused his cock to fill. He pulled back the long skin and a soft sigh escaped him.

He lay back, stroking himself as he thought about Anan. His pleasure was building when he heard.

"Terja?"

He frantically scrambled, knocking supplies to the ground as he struggled to cover himself. "Wait. Stay out."

Terja tightened the last lacing on his kilt and plunged through the cover. He'd hoped they didn't know, but the small smile on Anan's lips left little doubt that he knew exactly what Terja had been doing. Having been caught, his face felt close to igniting. "Sorry, I was cleaning up—" He studied Joven before glancing at Anan. He filled with questions, but none formed into words.

"Terja, this is Joven. He was—He helped me kill the first of our enemy and dispose of the body."

Terja scanned the young man. His velvet was matted with Twined Ones only knew what. Even with Anan's healing, the lash marks covering him were obviously inflamed. Terja remained frozen in place. Then he reached a decision and motioned them into the shelter. "I have food cooking, but you need to clean yourself. Anan is a spellweaver and can work on your… injury."

Joven nodded and eased through the brush. He followed Terja without a word and sat beside the pool. Terja caught Anan's gaze and flicked his eyes toward the cooking basket. Anan began heating the cooking stones in the coals while Terja dug in their packs. He found a small square of material scavenged from their village and dipped it into the pool. After squeezing out the excess water, he wiped at the bloody garrote wound around the youngster's neck. He moved over his chest and back, the water of the small pool darkening as he rinsed the filth and blood from the cloth. Terja reached the top of the filthy kilt and stopped.

Without a word, Joven stood, unlaced his kilt, and let it drop to the ground. Terja swallowed hard at the unveiled network of infected welts. He glanced at Anan, who never looked up from the meal he was cooking. Terja rinsed the cloth as best he could and handed it to Joven.

"You can clean the rest. I'm sure you don't want me touching you down…" He nodded to Joven's crotch.

Joven glanced at his naked body and shrugged, as if none of this mattered any more than a cloudflyer floating past. Terja bent down to retrieve the kilt when he noticed Joven had crawlers. The thought of the small biting creatures infesting their bedding made Terja's skin crawl. He backed away a step and turned to Anan. "You need to do a weaving for the crawlers he has."

Anan focused on the young man. The spell was simple. Terja had seen boys who had just came into their weaver's magic practicing it in the village. That a weaver had been so stripped of matama that he didn't have a thread left to do the simple spell told Terja how desperate the situation was for the captives. He picked up the foul kilt and started to wash out the filth. Anan was putting together the simple weaving to kill anything living on Joven or infesting the bit of clothing.

The wind shifted and blew from Joven to Terja, and he choked at the stench. Part wound poisoning and part days of neglect, few living things had offended his senses more. But as Joven washed, the smell lessened. Terja moved to the other side of the pool and scrubbed the garment. Time crawled past on their oddly domestic scene. By the time the stew was bubbling, Terja had finished cleaning Joven's clothing and laid it over a nearby branch to dry. Joven seemed oblivious to his nudity, so despite his discomfort, Terja decided to not mention it.

While they'd cleaned the young man and his clothing, Anan wove eating bowls for each of them. With just him and Terja, they'd eaten from the cooking basket. But with three of them, Terja agreed with Anan's decision to not use a communal bowl. He spooned out stew for each of them. Anan used the last of the dried food in this meal. *Tomorrow we'll have to hunt. The springtail I lost today would've been helpful.* He doubted Joven would be fit to help find food anytime soon. But at least they had enough for tonight.

Both he and Anan ate slowly as Joven's share of the stew disappeared with single-minded ferocity. Anan dished Joven a second helping, and Terja realized the extra came from Anan's own bowl, not the now empty cooking basket. Anan smiled at him when Terja snuck his portion of the stew back in so Anan could give Joven a little more. By the time the injured man ran his finger along the bottom of the dish to get the last drops, he no longer mimicked a starved longtooth.

Joven's eyes fluttered closed.

"Sorry, Joven, but you can't sleep yet. I need to weave more healing over those whip marks," Anan said.

Terja picked up the eating baskets and tossed them into the fire. Their few tools he washed in the clean water above the pool, which still looked dim and murky. By the time he'd spread their sleeping mats on the shelf, Anan seemed to have decided what needed to be done.

"Lay down. We need to do another weaving on your back and chest, or the wound poison will worsen. While your weaving stopped the bleeding, the wounds weren't cleaned right." He smiled. "But there are not many reasons for someone your age to have practiced them."

"Traitor."

Stunned for a moment, Anan asked, "What? I'm no traitor."

He shook his head. "No. The traitor did the healing. They said I was too scarred to be sold to a pleasure house and if I could be healed they would sell me to the sex pits."

Terja's gut twisted, and a strangled noise escaped from between his lips. He'd tried to hide his horror at the boy's treatment, but all the Talac knew of the terror of the pits. It was where the most addicted Varas used up the last bits of life from captive Talac. Blocking the thought from his mind, he turned to Joven. "What do you mean traitor?"

Joven gave him the blank look that was becoming familiar. "The weaver. I think his name is Xain. He's the reason the Varas can attack our villages instead of just capturing a few herdweavers before running back to their territory."

"A weaver. A weaver is working with the Varas." The fact still astounded Terja. But as he thought back on the past few days, he realized Anan had been right, they must have been worried someone was following them. There was no other way for the trails to be hidden as they were. And now that they'd discovered the Varas had a weaver who was working with them, several pieces fell into place. He still couldn't imagine what would make a weaver do this.

Joven continued, his voice flat and expressionless. "I don't know why he did it. Not why he is helping the Varas or why he healed me. They threw one of the Pero to the deathspinners, and Xain gave him mercy."

Terja shuddered at the thought of someone given to the lethal predators and another slave killing him in mercy.

Joven moved to lie down, and Terja ached at the sight of his abused body. Whoever'd beaten him was skilled, methodical, and incredibly sadistic. The scars left barely a fingertip of velvet unmarked. From ankle to neck, his skin was a network of festering lash marks. Terja couldn't imagine the pain or the determination he'd showed to simply move each day. Some of the recently closed strips of raw flesh had reopened in the short distance he and Anan had traveled. He didn't want to consider the amount of pain Joven was enduring.

96

Terja waited to hear Anan's assessment, but instead Anan opened his spellweaver's sight and began laying the matama for the healing. The first threads dulled the pain, and they disappeared into either side of Joven's neck. From there Terja knew Anan would be finding the worst of the wound fever and blocking the threads of disease. By the time Anan finished, the sun touched the treetops on the valley rim, but when Terja studied the work, he saw the thin lines of healing blue twined around every visible lash mark.

"How do you feel?" Anan asked.

Joven turned, and a tear rolled down his cheek. "The pain is gone. I'm sure I'll be fine now."

"You need to spend less time with the herds. I've only lessened the pain. I've barely begun the healing."

Joven flushed red, and he turned away as if to prepare for whatever was next. Terja looked at Anan and got a nod in return. He had harvested the threads of matama from the two of them for days, and now from the Varas camp. Terja had been pleased at Anan's amazement with the purity of the colors. He'd told Terja he'd never seen such vibrancy, not even from the elder spellspinners. Those were the spinnings that had been woven into their kilt panels. Both their kilts were now as intricately embellished as any clan leader's ceremonial garb. It was these matama that Anan would use on Joven.

Anan created a spellweaving large enough to cover the herdweaver from head to toe. The worst spots of wound fever would need more focused treatments, but his spell would heal the less severe places. As the last weft thread slipped into place along the iridescent warp, a surge of fresh power built inside Terja. He'd never been told of another pair with the ability to share raw matama. But since discovering the gift from First Twining, it continued to grow and develop. Now Terja fed the matama he gathered to Anan as easily as he would spin silk and matama together. Anan pulled a new surge of matama and fed them into the healing web and the lines of green pooling at the areas of the worst damage.

Joven sighed and sank into the sleeping mats.

"Don't move any more than absolutely needed. You might tear some of the injuries again. Each time the wound has to heal, it takes longer, and the scarring is worse," Terja said.

Joven looked apprehensive.

"Turn over," Anan said. "We need to deal with the rest of your wounds."

"Please. No. I think it's enough for now."

Anan looked puzzled at the sudden hesitancy. "No, we must do them all at the same time. Otherwise some of the connections could be damaged."

Joven's face twisted, and tears rolled down his cheeks. "Please. No."

Terja sighed with exasperation. "None of your scars are going to offend us."

With a shaking body, Joven turned over slowly. As his almost nonexistent hips rotated, his stone-hard cock sprung into view. Terja started to smile, but remembered this wasn't an innocent young man in the heat of mating. The Varas may have used him against his will, and his body may have responded in a way to avoid more beatings. That thought squelched any humor he found in the situation.

Anan and Joven's gazes locked. "It's perfectly normal. Weaving is sensual, and healing weaving is particularly so. You've done nothing to cause yourself shame."

The conversation seemed private, and Terja didn't want to make Joven any more uncomfortable than he already was. He busied himself cataloging their supplies while Anan checked the wounds covering Joven.

Anan touched the herdweaver as little as possible. He seemed careful to avoid anything that would embarrass Joven any further. Judging from the thick, clear stream coming from his shaft, Joven was close to orgasm, and Terja could only imagine the impact if that should happen.

Terja could clearly see Anan's second large weaving of the evening. The magic flowing through it was clear in Terja's spell sight. This weaving was larger and more detailed. Joven's organs and face presented a particular problem, but Anan worked quickly. He pulled the matama from the panels on his kilt, letting the healing greens flow where the spell thought it was needed most.

Joven tensed, and for a moment Terja feared they had triggered the event they'd hoped to avoid. Joven's cock jumped and threw off a particularly thick strand. Time crawled past, and Terja glanced toward Anan, and their gazes met as the faint sound of Joven moving to cover himself filled the space.

Terja stepped outside the cave and retrieved the still damp kilt from the bush where he'd hung it to dry. He held it out.

"It's still wet. But at least you have your kilt, so when it dries—"

Joven grabbed the wet kilt and wrapped it around his emaciated waist. He laced it quickly before walking to the opposite side of the cave to sit.

Anan studied him, realizing there would be no quick resolution with this one, and began their plans for the next day.

CHAPTER ELEVEN

TERJA SLICED the hindquarters of the daggerhorn into thin strips and hung them to one side of the fire. Their last few days had been spent spying on the Varas encampment and replenishing their food. Joven's voracious appetite made the second task more difficult. Anything Anan and Terja dug, gathered, or hunted became food for his unending hunger.

Chewing on a piece of dried meat, Joven stared at Anan. Since the healing, the young man had become obsessed with Anan. Over the days since his rescue, Joven became more mobile, and his responsibilities increased. Although his body was slowly recovering from the abuse, Joven's mind still seemed removed from this world, forcing Terja to give instructions as he would with a kit.

He shook his head at the young man they were burdened with. His mind seemed to have drifted into the aether, except for his obsession with Anan. Terja had seen the expression before. One of the other spinners had fallen for a boy in the clan, and she couldn't talk of anything but him. How he talked, how he walked, the skill of his weaving, and later, the skill of his lovemaking. Now Joven's obsession contained a similar weave. Even the few questions he asked were related to Anan.

They both looked up when Anan slipped through the brush with a brace of springtail. He laid them in front of Joven and smiled. "Dress these and put them on the spit for tonight." His lips curled into a feral smile. "Another Varas found out going too far from camp to release your water was a bad idea. The deathspinners and longtooth should love me."

An unfamiliar feeling twisted and built inside Terja when Joven picked up the springtail, ran his hand down Anan's chest, and beamed at him. "You are wonderful, weaver. Whoever twines with you is blessed."

Terja looked between the two, and a bitter taste filled his mouth. "The deathspinners already liked you, or we would not be alive. But I'm certain the Varas are aware they are under attack. Your easy targets will disappear soon."

Anan frowned as he stared into his gaze. "The Varas are preparing to move, and then everything will be much more difficult. Between your sling and my bow, we'll keep thinning their numbers. Since our spells are gaining in strength I'm thinking to weave some traps."

Terja considered the impending battle with the slavers. "Once we close with the Varas, the shield is all I have. I need to find a club or staff. I can use it with the training dances to hone my skills."

"Why don't you use the toothed staff?"

Both men looked at Joven. "What are you talking about?" Terja asked.

He fluttered his hands like a swarm of cloudflyers. "The staff Anan picked up after killing Hirvio. It's toothed."

Anan retrieved the object he'd picked up and studied it. A few moments later, he looked at Terja. "I don't know why I brought it back. It just seemed the right thing to do. But with everything else happening I had forgotten it."

Terja calmed himself as he took the weapon from Anan. He was braced for the shaft to be embedded with Varas matama. To his surprise none of their disjointed energies were hosted in the weapon. A moment longer and surprise filled him. "This is Talac."

Joven nodded in his absent way, as if he were no longer part of this world. "They attacked a Talac family away from their clan and killed them, except one with golden velvet. I heard the guards say he was valuable as a pleasure slave. They found the weapon. Soneri is his name. I think the staff was his." He paused as if recalling barely accessible information. "The old ones told stories of staffweavers, but the Kuri stopped using them many lifetimes ago. Hirvio cut the shaft shorter. Soneri is tall even for a Kuri, and you know the Varas are only a little taller than a kit just in his adult velvet."

"How do you know about the staffs?" Anan asked.

"The weaver who taught me insisted I know the history of each and every weave he knew. One of them was a useless spell to fuse a tooth to its shaft. But you need something he called deathglue. And he didn't know what it was. But that's a toothed staff." He motioned to the object. "It fits his description exactly."

Terja turned the blade in his hand. The head was bound to the staff by wrapping a wet hide tightly around it and letting it dry. The wrap created a tight joint, but not perfect. *Something isn't right. What am I missing?* He narrowed his eyes at Joven. "Who used a toothed staff?"

He returned a tired glance. "Only the spellspinners. They knew the patterns of death the tooth could deliver. That's what he said anyway."

The image of his practice staff came to Terja, the heavy weight at one end his father could only say was tradition. He hefted the toothed staff in his hand. It might have been close to the same weight, but the shaft was far too short for the patterns he'd been taught. And the glue… why did the glue seem so familiar?

"The eggs."

Terja's head snapped up, and his gaze locked with Anan, who repeated himself. "The eggs. The fiber spheres. They're the source of the deathglue."

Terja's face became a grim convergence of emotions. "There are ironwood trees close." His voice brooked no question.

A SOFT touch the following morning awoke Anan. His first thought was of Silbre, and his second of Terja. He found reality far more disturbing. The touch was Joven. The young man's hard and urgent cock pressed against his side. He moved as if they were lovers, but the thought held no appeal for Anan. He might have seen Joven as a younger brother, a friend of sorts, but never a lover.

He caught Joven's gaze, hoping he simply acted out a dream. But the amber eyes that met his were filled with desire. Any doubt disappeared. He wanted to share pleasures. Anan struggled to find a way to reject his advances without hurting the young man's damaged self-worth. He put his hands against Joven's chest and pushed them apart.

"Joven. No."

Joven whimpered, trying to grind himself against Anan. "You call me. All night. I must have you."

"Joven. This isn't going to happen. You're like a brother. But we're not destined to be twined or even share pleasures."

He ran his hand over Anan. If the touch had been Terja's, his response would have been far different, but from the former captive, the touches caused nothing more than concern. Joven's gaze filled with an unnatural emptiness. His worry built when the empty blankness that had lived inside Joven since he was rescued deepened. *I've never given him any reason to think a connection existed between us. Why does he think we're lovers?*

When realization came, it was almost too late. He cast the weaving he'd been taught to keep ready as his own blade slid into his belly. The weaving slipped into place while the agony overwhelmed him. He could see Joven's face above him as he grabbed at his stomach. The world spun and then went black.

His eyes fluttered open, and this time Terja's face filled his vision. Terja trembled, his hands shaking as they touched. Anan glanced around to see what happened to Joven. "Is he dead?"

Terja shook his head. "No, it was close, though. He almost became the first blooding for the toothed staff. Lucky for him, your weaving stunned him. I heard what you told him and was prepared. At least enough to use the butt of the staff to knock him unconscious."

Anan sighed with relief, just before a wave of agony from his belly wound brought a gasp.

"Be still," Terja said. "I'm no weaver. I've stopped the worst bleeding, but it's not done as a weaver would heal it."

"Is there…."

Terja shook his head. "There was no scent of bowel. I think you will heal." Terja smiled at Anan. "Especially if you check my work."

He grabbed Terja's shoulder. "Thank you. If it weren't for you, I'd be dead." He glanced over as Joven started to awaken. He cocked an eyebrow, and this time the weaving he used was more than a protective shell. He wove the spell used by healers to send the person into a deep sleep and strengthened it with corcra. Anan anchored the warp threads deeply in the aether for the strongest effect. Joven dropped unmoving against the rock floor, and Anan enjoyed a sweet satisfaction at the hollow thud his head made upon impact. He turned back to Terja as weakness overwhelmed him.

"He'll be asleep the rest of the night. My spell was particularly strong with this weaving."

"Good. I'd regret pounding his head each time he awakened." Terja grinned. "Hold still and let me see if I can't spin the wound shut." Terja took the fibers in the depth of the cut and spun them against each other. Anan clenched his teeth as Terja's work progressed, sealing the larger blood vessels as he went. By the time he finished, sweat drenched Anan's velvet. Terja paused and took in a shuddering breath.

"Wait. I need to flush it with matama to clear any wound poison," Anan said.

Terja nodded and sat back on his heels as Anan wove a tight and intense spell. He ground his teeth together as he released the spell into the wound. A groan of pain escaped when the weaving created the sensation of someone shoving a hot iron into his gut. The pain washed over Anan, but as his vision began to narrow, the agony stopped. With a sigh of relief, he collapsed into the bedding, gasping for air.

His vision swam for a few moments, and he closed his eyes to keep from losing his last meal. When he reopened them, Terja sat beside him, holding a bowl of stew. He gave a concerned smile as he held the food out to Anan. "Here. Eat something. You lost a lot of blood before I could close the severed veins." Terja shook his head. "If you'd been a single heartbeat slower, he would have sunk the knife into your organs. I doubt either of us have enough matama to heal that injury."

"It's not his fault." Anan paused for a moment. "At least I don't think it is. We'll see once he awakens. I think whoever did his healing set a trap. I had hoped they weren't aware of us, but it appears I was wrong. Or it was a blind trap to kill anyone who tried to save him. Tonight wasn't the youngster we've been caring for over the past few days. I think the trap was hidden in all the other wound poisons."

Terja nodded and twisted his lips, his brows furrowed. "If he had succeeded in hurting you badly, he would have died. I don't care what motives were planted in him."

His fervor surprised Anan. He knew his feelings for Terja were deepening but hadn't known the spinner might have equally strong emotions toward him. He studied Joven. "Help me up. I want to take a look at the weaving on him before he wakes."

"First let me close the wound. Unless you think you can weave it shut yourself," Terja said and cocked an eyebrow.

Anan started to argue but realized he didn't have enough strength for any more healing. "All right. Spin it closed, then. I'll proudly wear a spinner's ridge for the rest of my life."

Terja frowned but began the work. Other than a tension on Anan's stomach and the light touch of Terja's fingers, the process was painless. By the time Terja finished, a small portion of Anan's strength had returned. He checked the work to find a tiny ridge where a gaping hole had been earlier.

"That's amazing. Many weavers couldn't have closed the skin so skillfully."

Terja flushed, his face going pink to Anan's amusement. "I wanted you to have as little scarring as possible. It would seem the gifts of the Twined Ones continue to unwind."

"Well, it's skillfully done. Now, help me get over to Joven so I can see if we should let him live."

Terja looked like he was going to argue. Then Anan cocked an eyebrow. Seemingly resigned to Anan's demands, Terja moved behind him and slid his hands under Anan's arms. He caught scent of Terja's concern, evidence their connection had deepened past anything he'd heard of before. Terja ducked under Anan's arm to give him support, and the two of them moved to Joven's side.

Anan studied the now peaceful young man. He'd never thought Joven would try to murder him. When he looked down, a shade of guilt flitted over him at the small pool of blood where Joven hit his head. Anan let his vision slide into place. He saw the familiar network of scars and infection. This time he knew the latticework in the skin hid a much more malicious weaving. He traced the threads numerous times and found nothing. The weaving telling Joven to kill him existed inside the young man somewhere, but he couldn't find the elusive compulsion. Anan was beginning to doubt the existence of a trap, when he spotted a dissonant thread. It wrapped around the network of pathways traveling up and down Joven's spine, virtually invisible.

He began to tease at the angry filament, careful never to break the fragile thread that wandered into every part of Joven's body. As he unraveled the spell, he forced down his anger. If he failed to remove any fragment, they would have to kill Joven to protect themselves. They couldn't risk everything to try to save Joven. Anan locked his emotions and doubts away, sending his entire being into the unweaving. The sun dipped just above the western horizon when the pattern began to materialize.

Anan's chest tightened. He recognized the weaving style; it was from their clan. But he couldn't remember any lost Kuri. As nightfall deepened, he reached the end of his endurance. Fortunately, he was finished.

Anan breathed a sigh of relief when he reached the end of the thread. But a tremor of shock traveled through his body when he found the tip of a guardian thorn at the end of the pattern. Somehow the weaver who set the trap managed to neutralize the poison and use the tip as a lethal trigger. The thorn was set to begin moving and pierce a large blood vein at the base of Joven's neck if someone attempted to heal him. Ingenious, and insidious. It would have punctured the vein in a few days, and Anan would have thought a random accident with the thorn killed him. Otherwise it would have probably lasted the brief remainder of Joven's life.

He wove the tip out after encasing each barb in weaving. He guided the tip to the surface, and soon it materialized as a white blister. Anan paused to consider his options before noting Terja's presence. When Anan glanced toward him, Terja held out the obsidian knife to Anan.

The spinner's clenched jaws made Anan wonder about his intent. Terja nodded toward the white pocket. "Cut it out. I don't see another way. If you push it through, the wrappings might rupture. We don't know if anything else is hidden in the tip."

Anan considered the options for a moment. "You're right. Let's do it while he's still asleep."

He pressed the tip of the knife against the spot on the young man's neck. The skin parted easily, and he used the blade to lift out the knot with the thorn tip. He dropped it into the fire and staggered back a step when it flared as the spell's unidentifiable matama dissolved into the aether.

He peered into the flames before smiling at Terja. "I think we got everything. Just a purge weaving, and then I'm going to rest."

Anan wove the healing matama that he hoped would destroy the malicious thread and anything he might have missed. The fire and ice from the weaving ran down the thread and turned the foreign filament into bits of dust. The destruction of the thread brought a low moan from Joven as his body shook and his back arched. Terja looked at him and lifted an eyebrow.

"The web was everywhere. It looked like the seed was the thorn tip, and then it grew lethal roots through Joven's system. I'm sure its destruction was painful. But the healing would have been torture if he'd been awake." Anan gave Terja a slight smile. "You'll have to forgive me if I enjoyed his discomfort."

"No more than I am. And he won't recall what happened later."

"Oh, he will be sore. But that's it. Not much, considering."

They watched until Joven fell into a deep sleep. Anan realized they had worked until late in the night. He sighed with exhaustion. "I don't suppose you have more of the stew left?"

Terja picked up the cooking basket and handed it to him. "Eat. We'll sleep once you've set a weaving around us."

"A weaving? With a rogue Talac?"

"Yes, even with the traitor close. It won't be him who'll discover us."

Anan began to eat, the stew disappearing quickly as he discovered how hungry he was. As he ate, he created the weaving they needed, again using the trees surrounding them as the support of their weft threads. By the time he finished the perimeter web, his eyes were too heavy to keep open. Terja guided him to their sleeping mats, and they fell asleep as soon as their heads touched the bedding.

Anan woke the next morning with a sensation he hadn't experienced since the last time he slept with Silbre: the weight of an arm across his chest, holding him tight and protecting him. He relaxed and let the memory blend with reality. He ran his hand down the body behind him, enjoying the smooth side and thigh.

Anan froze. This was the spinner. Terja held him tight. What frightened him most was... it felt good. He found the embrace comforting, and he had never expected to find comfort again after losing Silbre. Terja wriggled closer, and his warmth flowed into Anan. Unlike Joven's attempted seduction, this touch caused a rising heat. Terja might have issues with weavers, but his embrace radiated a wonderful pleasure Anan intended to relish. Like someone cared about him again.

He moved, and Terja rustled behind him. With a rumbling voice he said, "Morning, Anan." In a half-awake movement, he leaned in and kissed the back of Anan's neck. The warmth and scent of ardor built, and then he realized what he'd done.

"Oh, ravelings, I'm so sorry, Anan. I didn't intend.... But I was... I thought I was going to lose... then...."

Anan chuckled and twisted in Terja's arms until they faced each other. He trapped Terja's face between his hands, leaned forward, and kissed him gently. "Today was the best way I've woken up since... since my thread with Silbre was cut."

"I'm sorry, Anan. I did not intend to overstep boundaries. I know I am not Silbre."

"I will always miss Silbre. But he would not want me to spend the rest of my life alone. I'm not ready to take a new twining, but your touch makes me want more. We might not be alive tomorrow. I think the Twined Ones will understand if we take what comfort we can from each other."

"Anan, I am not…."

"Shh. Do you enjoy my touch?"

Terja smiled, slid his hands over Anan's plush body, and traced the dark swirls covering him. His hands trembled at the sensations under his palm. "Yes, you make my body shake, and fire floods me. But you know I've never been with anyone. What if you don't enjoy yourself?" After a moment he motioned toward Joven. "And what if he wakes?"

Anan planted another kiss on his cheek. "I don't care, but the weaving was strong enough to keep him from waking before midday. Your lack of experience isn't a problem." Anan winked at Terja. "You won't know if I'm inept."

HE STARTED to explain again, but Anan pushed him onto his back and lay across his chest. The luscious sensation of his velvet-covered chest ignited a wildfire in Terja, and he lost all will to resist. His cock filled in an instant, and he ached for a touch. He gasped as the weaver kissed along his neck. The slight tickle of Anan's lips sent jolts of pleasure over his nerves. He loosened the laces of Anan's kilt and opened the covering as the fabric slipped to either side of his torso. His own kilt quickly followed, leaving them both bare.

When he moved his mouth down Terja's chest, his breath caught. The flicker of Anan's tongue across his nipple sent a jolt of lightening to his groin. He convulsed, and his cock slapped against his stomach.

Anan slowed his advance until he came to a stop, smiling and then pressing their lips against each other. "Perhaps if you touch me. Hopefully the sensations are not as new and potent for me."

He felt excitement at the opportunity to explore Anan. He was drawn as strongly as cloudflyers were to mountain flowers. He straddled the handsome man, pushed his arms over his head, and nuzzled along his neck. The action enveloped him in Anan's musk. The scent charged his system with desire.

In a moment of hesitation, he glanced at Anan. His reply came in the form of a nod. Granted permission, Terja pressed his face into Anan's armpit and inhaled deeply. The scent of the man curled into his nose, and a flood of desire again filled his body. He shook as the emotions scorched through his system, and then moved toward Anan's nipples, his tongue darting out to taste each one. But this time he wanted more, so he turned to Anan's pulsing cock.

He looked again for confirmation.

"Do what you want. If you think you want to try something, then go ahead. I'll probably enjoy it too. Nothing is off-limits."

"But what if I do something you don't enjoy?"

"I swear to tell you if that happens."

A measure of confidence filled him, and he eased his hand over Anan's skin, again luxuriating in the sensation. He slid his fingertips closer, until they traced one of the veins running up the side of Anan's cock. With a shuddering breath from the weaver, a single clear drop appeared at the tip. He hesitated for a moment, then ran his tongue over Anan's slit. A flavor reminiscent of musk and smelling of the grasslands filled Terja's senses. He skirted the deep red crown with his tongue and then swiped the new droplet forming at its tip. Anan spun Terja and took him between his lips. The combined sensation of them sucking each other's cocks was driving Terja closer to climax.

Terja became lost in teasing and licking Anan's cock. His body moved closer and closer to the edge as a banquet of flavors filled him. He gasped when a jolt of pleasure shot through him with the force of a summer grassfire. Anan ran his tongue over Terja's rock-hard cock a second time. His body's response was no less charged. Terja's mind whirled with ecstasy, building with each pass of Anan's tongue. His feelings for the velvet-covered weaver grew.

Terja dove onto Anan's dick and mirrored each of Anan's moves with his own. He fought back the building climax as he stroked and licked at Anan's cock. The sensation changed as Anan pressed his lips around Terja's shaft and took its length. Anan's masculine scent served as the final push, and his orgasm began. Terja felt his seed race for release and struggled to pull Anan off.

His body shuddered as the first stream of white launched. Several additional waves followed the first, each creating its own unique thread of pleasure. Terja's body convulsed, his muscles contracting and releasing joy. This time was different from their first, and he wanted to return the euphoria he'd been given.

He slid his body over Anan's. The sensation of his bare skin slipping over Anan's velvet created a lightning storm of ecstasy. As he rode the final wave of his climax, he took one of Anan's hard nipples between his teeth. He flicked his tongue across the nub of flesh and enjoyed the rumble of pleasure from Anan.

Terja relished his time while the world around them lightened. Their life-weavings intertwined, and the connection went beyond physical pleasures. A series of low moans came from Anan as Terja began to move down his luscious body. He slid lower until he sat on Anan's crotch and could feel their hard cocks against each other. The sensation of cock rubbing up and down the cleft of his butt brought new pleasure to Terja. The heat of their crotches grinding together built, and from the soft moans it seemed the passion was shared. Terja wanted more; his hunger was like nothing he'd experienced before. He slid lower on Anan's legs and pressed his hand against his full crotch.

He rubbed Anan's cock and trapped it against his firm abdomen. Anan's cock twitched as if it had a mind of its own, hovering above his stomach, a clear stream running from its tip. He reached down and cupped Anan's balls, letting them slip between his fingers, fascinated by their weight. He glanced up to see a smile stretched across his face.

"That feels good. Perfect," Anan said.

Terja smiled, the heat of embarrassment, and pleasure, filling him at the compliment. The self-imposed pressure to please lessened, and Terja worked to explore more of the weaver's body.

He lowered himself between Anan's legs and wrapped his hand around his cock. A rumbling sigh came from the man under him, and the stream from his dick surged out to run down the shaft. Terja leaned close, ran his tongue over the slit, and savored the faint musk.

Anan's foreskin extended further than his, and he found himself fascinated. He gripped the skin between his teeth and tugged, then flicked his tongue under the hood of flesh. Taking advantage of the chance, he toyed with the ample skin for several moments. Terja gripped low on Anan's hard shaft and slid the skin higher until it covered the tip. Anan's breath came harder when Terja lowered his face and then slipped his tongue inside to tease the crown.

He remembered the sensations Anan had created, and wanted to do the same. Dropping his head, Terja sank lower until the crown of Anan's cock pressed against the back of his throat. He pulled backward, enjoying the sensation as he eased his mouth up and down the length. Anan's groans drove Terja to increase his speed.

Terja glanced toward him, afraid something was wrong, only to find bliss filling Anan's face. His weakly flailing hands pulled at Terja, but he had no intention of being deprived of this treat. When his tongue dug into the underside of Anan's cock, the first blast flooded his mouth.

He swallowed quickly, trying to keep it all but losing some of the massive climax. White cream dribbled from the corners of Terja's lips as he nursed the load. Anan's cock flexed a last time, and he drew in the final drops. Terja circled the cockhead with his tongue before twisting away.

"No more. You have me in agony as it is," Anan said with a contented grumble. He pulled Terja upward until their eyes met and leaned forward to lick his essence from the edge of Terja's mouth. He separated them and smiled, then leaned in again for their lips to caress. Anan rolled them so he was on top and slipped between his legs. He pressed his face against Terja's crotch and inhaled deeply. An instant later, he sucked the drooling shaft between his lips and pressed down. In one smooth unbroken motion, Anan swallowed its entire length. Terja shuddered as the muscles of Anan's throat rippled down his hard length again and again. He moved closer to the edge with each pass when Anan pulled off. He whimpered and curled up to see Anan's smiling face as he slid his hand up and down his cock.

"You stopped! Oh by the Spinner! Don't stop."

"But the build-up makes the ending even better."

Terja collapsed into their bedding and moaned, lost in the sensations. The heat built as he squirmed. His ecstasy grew to a new high, and Anan swallowed his cock again. Terja's body tensed, and a ripple of lightning washed over him as he plunged into euphoria. Their connection deepened as his body tensed and released time and again until he braced himself against Anan and shook. When the final wave of pleasure washed over him, he collapsed into their bedding. A few moments later, Anan lay beside him and pressed their bodies together.

They lay quiet and drifted from their respective states of bliss. He wanted nothing more than to lie with Anan. The thought of separation left him with a hollowness. He rolled to his side and rested his hands on Anan.

Anan turned to him. "Are you all right? Was sharing a mistake?"

He inhaled the delicious scent of Anan's body and could sense their matama blending in ways his teachers never talked about. After kissing Anan's bicep he settled in next to him. "Our intimacy was better than anything I could have imagined." Joven shifted in his sleep, and Terja glanced toward the young man. "What are we going to do with him?"

Anan followed his gaze. "Watch him. It might grow again. If I keep working on the wounds, finding the spell will be easier. But that could take days, maybe more than we can spare."

"So we guard against him every night?"

Anan held up their kilts for Terja to see. The new spell panels Anan had woven on each of them were shot through with tones of purple. He met Terja's gaze. "I've never known of a spinner before who can blend fibers without focusing on them. But it's good for

Joven. We have enough corcra to weave him into a deep sleep every night for the next moon."

"You wove corcra to put Joven out? What will it do to him?"

"The alternative is to cut his throat."

He paused, then glanced at Anan and saw he was deathly serious. They didn't know enough about the spell that had caused Joven to try to kill Anan to understand what was possible. The bloodweaving came first. The captives had to be rescued. He nodded and sighed. "You're right. This is the evil the Varas left us. We're forced to consider taking the life of another Talac in order to fulfill our pledge."

"Let's wake Joven and see. Perhaps we can tell more once he's conscious." He moved a few steps and was stopped by a chuckle. He glanced back to see Terja holding out his kilt.

"I think you might want this."

CHAPTER TWELVE

ANAN DEFTLY set the trap, laying a weaving for the trigger. The Varas knew someone hunted them now, and picking off one or two at a time became more and more difficult. But he continued to scatter them through areas where he thought Varas might travel, like the current glade. Between ambushes and traps, half the Varas were dead.

Joven had been horrified when they'd told him his body had been spelled. The thought of what he'd almost done made him vomit. He willingly, almost eagerly, allowed the sleep weaving each evening. Anan could see no lasting effect of the corcra, which he and Terja enjoyed replenishing.

When they first discovered the Varas, the slavers had been moving quickly, which made Anan's trickery more difficult. Now they moved cautiously and much slower. If they suspected traps, they used the Talac captives to check. Their new tactic meant the traps had to be easily spotted by anyone with even the barest level of sight. He finished the simple springtail snare he was crafting and studied his work. This time the noose was full of guardian thorns. If they set off the trap, the Varas would have more lethal thorns buried in them than the spines on a rattleback.

He glanced up to the increasingly common sight of Terja guarding him and Joven hovering on the edge of the clearing. This particular opening in the forest giants had been formed when a summer hell-bringer storm toppled one of the ancient ironwood trees. The frantic scramble for light resulted in a carpet of young trees on the forest floor. As a result, hundreds of tall, straight saplings perfect for snare springs grew, and the cover was dense enough to hide the triggers from Varas eyes. A perfect setup.

He waved Terja and Joven closer as they made their way into the brush. The youngster moved more quietly than Terja, but only slightly. Anan was uneasy in the dense growth. It could hide a Varas attack as easily as his snares.

The sense of unease increased as they moved along the edge of the forest. Terja grumbled, but Anan forced them to stay in the deepest cover. His senses detected nothing, but he feared the strain of constant weaving might be taking a toll on the strength of his spell vision.

A twig snapped, and the faint noise echoed through the air. His head and bow swung in unison, releasing the arrow within a heartbeat of the sound. It pierced the skull of a Varas just as his quarrel slammed into Anan's shoulder. He dropped to a crouch, fighting to block the burning pain, as he scanned for more of the ambushing Varas.

Grim satisfaction filled him at the sound of an unfamiliar voice screaming. Terja had blooded his toothed staff. Then several men surged at him. He braced himself against the pain and released two arrows in rapid succession. Feathered shafts quickly sprouted from two men's chests. When another stopped to take aim, Anan planted an arrow through his eye.

Anan spun toward the sound of running feet to find a Varas brandishing his knife. With no time to nock an arrow, Anan swung his ironwood bow and heard a satisfying crunch as it made contact with the Varas's face.

Another Varas rushed Terja and went down with a ruined throat from a skillful motion of Terja's staff. Close behind another attacker burst from the cover, and Terja threw his staff, burying it deep in the slaver's chest.

Anan dropped to his knees as the pain and bleeding took their toll. He glanced up in time to see a twisted face staring at him over the top of a crossbow. The twang from the quarrel's release signaled Anan's death.

A spray of blood covered Anan. Joven stood between them with an oddly peaceful expression and a crossbow bolt protruding from his chest.

"Did it," Joven gasped out before he fell forward.

Anan caught him, cradling his limp body as his eyes locked on the Varas working to reload his crossbow. Anan reached for his bow, only to discover a broken bowstring from when it was used as a club. He saw the delight on the Varas's face when he realized Anan was defenseless.

A gurgling sound came from Joven, and Anan knew the young man in his arms was close to death. The Varas snapped the crossbow to his shoulder. *Soon I will be joining Joven.*

A scream of rage ripped across the opening as Terja called akhir. He grabbed the matama of the attacker and ripped them to him.

The Varas froze in place, his expression first one of confusion, then surprise as Terja stripped him of life energies. Then the pain of having his soul ripped into fragments created a silent scream.

The look of fury and determination registered on Terja's face as the tips of his fingers blackened from the backlash. Anan trembled, feeling Terja's impending death. But Joven sucked in another gurgling breath and drew him back. He knew he could never save Joven, but at least he could make him comfortable. He began to weave.

Fighting back tears, he battled against the will of the Twined Ones. He created a weaving from instinct unlike any seen in many lifetimes. He quickly drained his kilt, and when he reached for more he hit the raw spinning coming to him through his connection with Terja. He tugged the thread to him and followed his weaver sight into Joven's chest. The weaving quickly slowed the bleeding, restitching severed veins. A whirlwind of matama flowed around the quarrel shaft, and the wooden fibers fell away. The space between Anan and Terja crackled and shone iridescent in the afternoon light as he lost himself in the healing. Time stopped as Terja stripped the last filaments from the Varas, and the husk of a body collapsed on the ground.

Anan realized the flow of threads had ended, and cut off his pull from Terja. *Terja? How is he alive? By the Great Weaving, he shouldn't be.* At that moment, Joven's body arched in a massive convulsion, and he sucked in air. He stared at the blood-drenched young man in time to see Joven's eyes flutter open.

Joven focused for a moment and then asked in a raspy voice, "What happened?"

Terja dropped to his knees beside them and then glanced to the unmoving corpse of the final Varas attacker before looking at Joven again.

"I have no idea," Anan said.

TERJA RUBBED his fingertips together, amazed he still lived. Even more astounding, his injuries were healed. He heard a low moan and glanced to the other miracle of the day, Joven. Anan fared the worst of the three of them and looked it. He was drenched in blood and had the remains of the crossbow bolt protruding from his shoulder. Terja and Joven carried Anan to the camp. Strangely enough, Joven acted more alive than anytime since they rescued him, as if being brought from the edge of death changed him.

He shifted his gaze to Joven as the herdweaver created the healing for Anan's shoulder, but he could find no criticism for Joven's skill. Terja spun him enough thread to heal Anan, but no more. The young weaver worked to remove the crossbow bolt. Fortunately the quarrel pierced only muscle, which made the healing much simpler, and Joven seemed confident of what needed to be done. He had already cut off the barbed iron head so he could remove the shaft.

When Joven began to work the shaft out, he handed Anan a stick to bite down on. The removal of the shaft would be bloody and painful from what Terja could see. The connection between him and Anan transmitted a shadow of the pain to Terja.

He froze. Their connection flared more strongly. The other times he could discount the sensations as something temporary. But now? Anan's pain rushed into him. Only a few of the pairings he'd known experienced a comparable level of intertwining. *We are not twined. This should not be happening.* He shifted to spinning sight and found the union easily. His awareness ran down its length, and he regretted his timing when Joven yanked out the shaft. Anan grunted around the stick, and his pain washed over Terja.

He recoiled, catching himself as the pain crested and began to ease. Sweat ran down his body when he fought to block the torment. A few heartbeats passed before the agony lessened. As he regained the ability to see, he found himself staring at Anan.

"We're connected. The same connection as only the strongest twined pairs have," said Terja.

"Yes."

"What does that mean?"

"You know what it means. You don't need me to explain."

"That's impossible. We were never twined. We didn't do any of the rituals. We cannot be paired. We've only—" He glanced at Joven but continued. "We've only made corcra."

Before Anan could answer, Joven moved in and silently prodded the injury. Anan remained immobile except for the muscles of his jaws clenching and unclenching as Joven checked the wound. He inhaled deeply and then slowly released the breath before he locked eyes with Terja again. His gaze left no room for denial. "We are twined, Terja. And the weaving between us is different than the one with Silbre. It's…." Anan paused, at a loss for words.

"Strong. Powerful," Joven said quietly. He looked at the small white scar in the middle of his chest that appeared to have healed years ago. "Very powerful."

Terja slipped into spinner's vision, studying again the thread running between them. A slight glimmer ran down its length, but it was no bigger than the finest of the deathspinner silk. He shifted closer and to his shock found the tether was woven. The number of threads creating the connection were too numerous to count when he shifted to an even closer view. Terja prepared to dive deeper into their binding to satisfy his growing fascination. But something grabbed him by the scruff of the neck and yanked backward.

Terja tumbled in darkness for a moment before the first whisper of wind crossed his sweat-drenched skin. When the world swam slowly into being around him, he found Anan kneeling in front of him. "Are you all right? I almost lost you. You can't go that deep and return. The threads will weave you into their fibers."

"I've never seen so many colors," Terja said.

"Neither have I. But it's active." He gave Terja a piercing look. "And very strong, ceremony or not."

The gravity of their discovery left Terja shaking. He was coming to terms with his attraction to Anan. But a twining? With Anan? The idea overwhelmed Terja to the point that he walled it away.

Terja motioned with his chin. "How are you? Considering all of us should be dead, you seem to have the most serious injury."

Anan rotated his shoulder slowly, a grimace flickering over his face a few times, but ending with a grim smile. "Not bad. I can pull a bow. Although I'd like to have more than a single day to heal."

"What happened? The akhir had begun. The tips of my fingers were burned. Then it stopped."

Anan sat unmoving for a handful of breaths, then nodded toward Joven. "I took matama from you to save him. I just remember pulling and suddenly having an unlimited supply. I used it to weave the injuries shut. Then everything is hazy."

Joven picked up the weft of the story. "Everything was going black, when suddenly it felt like I'd been hit with a second crossbow bolt. My sight blurred as a second wave went through me. Then… nothing. Not until I awoke with Anan holding me and covered in blood."

Terja turned to Anan. "Only in the old tales do spinners survive akhir."

"It seems the old tales are coming to life." He looked at Terja with a smirk. "But let's not try it again."

With a soft snort Terja said, "I agree."

GEIR LOOKED at the pale corpse in front of him and seethed. The body was ghastly. Something had stripped all color from the dead man. He looked like a slice of tallow from one of the grazing animals kept by the Varas herders. The man's eyes were white, the centers completely gone. Geir spun on Kotu and Xain.

"Talac did this?"

Xain nodded. "This is akhir. A spellspinner killed him."

Kotu grew dangerously still. "He will pay for this."

"He's dead."

Geir narrowed his eyes and stared at Xain. "And how would you know this, slave? Take care you answer correctly."

Xain looked first at him and then Kotu. Geir's rage was building before Xain spoke a word. But he recognized the cause as fear. Every Varas knew the story-fables of the horrible deaths of Varas at the hands of the Talac. Everyone knew they were animals mimicking intelligence, otherwise why would the gods give them pelts? Yes, every village had a few peltless ones that had neither pelts nor markings, ones they called spinners, but no Varas ever understood what it meant to be peltless, other than how they could kill. Even willing, pliable Xain couldn't explain, but he'd been sold to the Varas when he was young.

"It's the last spell of a spinner, akhir. The spinning strips the one they attack of... everything. Their being. And leaves them colorless."

"And the spinner?" asked Geir, his teeth grinding.

"They roast. Like an overcooked springtail. First the tips of their fingers, then up their arms, and sometimes to the rest of their bodies. But they all sacrifice themselves rather than be captured."

Geir looked at Xain and lifted an eyebrow. "But you allowed yourself to be taken. What's wrong, Xain? Did you not have the courage for this akhir?"

Xain drew himself upward and looked at Geir, expressionless. "I was barely an adolescent when my parents sold me to a Varas trader. They were banished from their clan and didn't follow the way of the Talac. Besides, weavers cannot do akhir."

Their eyes locked for a moment, and then Xain dropped his to the ground, his shoulder heaving.

"Get rid of the carrion, Xain. But we will also talk more about how this spinner escaped the irresistible trap you laid, without you knowing it."

SONERI LISTENED closely to the conversation between the Varas and the doubly hated Xain. He glanced over to see Morea propped against a small tree. After Joven's execution, she had been inconsolable. He forced her to eat and walked beside her when they moved so she didn't hurt herself. She saw him watching. She eased across the open area and squatted close to Soneri.

"What did you hear?" Morea asked.

"One of the Varas died from akhir. They don't know what that means. But for us it's one less rescuer."

"Couldn't they have lived?"

"No. Spinners don't survive akhir. The old stories are just that—stories."

One of the guards came close. They watched Soneri now after he'd tried to end his own life with an obsidian shard. But his velvet was worth almost as much as he was. The Varas's House of the Sun enjoyed many perversions. But he didn't want the guards to understand the two of them helped each other. When he did die, he didn't want Morea to suffer because of their friendship. It forced him to keep up the appearance that she was an annoyance to protect her, even though each time he was forced to do it the act broke him a little more.

"Get out of here, Kuri. You smell of your animals," Soneri said.

Morea should have left for another part of the slave enclosure; she wasn't on the chain that tethered the rest of them. Instead she began a laugh that was tinged with hysteria.

"I've been dragged off the grasslands to be a slave for some warped Varas for more than a moon. My velvet is filled with crawlers. We haven't been allowed to bathe in days, and I'm filthy beyond belief. I would welcome the fresh scent of a healthy kuri. I would gladly spend a season watching the herds with no complaint."

122

Soneri glanced to check the location of the guard and saw he'd moved away. He wasn't even sure their ruse worked. With a resigned sigh, he tucked the small girl against him.

"Kotu said there were a lot of wounded Talac, and they disappeared into the forest?" Morea asked.

"Yes, but Kotu lies. I doubt there was more than a handful. The Varas ran in fear."

"Shh. Keep your voice down."

Soneri started to argue and then thought better. Two of the men wrapped the Varas's body and carried it into the forest. They gave their own dead no more ceremonies than they did the bodies of the Talac. How could a people live who cared so little about the Great Weaving?

The two of them sat quietly for several minutes before they began to speak again.

"The spinner is dead," Soneri said.

"Yes, but...."

Soneri rested his hand on Morea's shoulder. "Yes, there might be more." He arched his brows as he glanced at Morea. A long missing feeling of vindication wound its way through Soneri. "There seem to be fewer Varas lately."

Morea stared at him, her mouth forming an O. But then she shook her head. "It can't be. We'll never be rescued."

Soneri shrugged. "It's the Twined Ones' will."

JOVEN SLITHERED through the low brush and grass along the edge of the bluff. They'd followed the slavers for days, and the Varas had become remarkably accident prone, all fatal. The local animals also deemed them prey. One even managed to corner a daggerhorn and be gored. They'd already been attacked once, so the Varas knew they were there. But Anan wanted them to continue secret attacks as long as possible.

Joven's personal concerns were the captives, especially Morea. He'd been relieved when he realized the gold velvet Talac protected her. He seemed to make sure she received her share of their meager rations and carried her when they moved. One thing surprised Joven. The gestures of defiance seemed to be more tolerated from this particular Talac.

He'd asked Anan for an explanation and had been surprised when the first question was the color of his velvet. When he'd told Anan it was light, he'd nodded and explained his worth to certain Varas.

As Joven looked at the confident figure again, he couldn't keep from wondering what he would do if their situations were reversed. The answer came to Joven: he knows. The light-colored one knew he was just as valuable dead as alive so long as he was unmarked. Everyone knew stories of the perverse fascination of some Varas for Talac pelts. He'd heard the guards speculating on the values of some of the Talac while he was a captive. A soft scuffing sound of Terja joining him shook Joven from his introspection.

Their gazes met, and Terja moved to the edge and began harvesting matama. The energy of the camp had built to the point Terja could easily gather energy to spin with the silk without the traitor realizing what was being done. Joven looked at his kilt panels that Anan renewed every night. It contained all the colors of flame. He'd never heard of a battle kilt before, but no other term existed for what he wore. Terja and Anan had worked together to create them, and now he and Anan worked to learn how to use the fiery breath of battle matama.

He moved off the path as Terja crawled back. Once they were side by side, Terja whispered, "Their guardian weaving is over two body lengths tall. They know they are under attack." He glanced at Joven again and motioned toward their back trail. As they moved away from the cliff, a numbing scream echoed around them. They flattened themselves, trying to sense where it originated. A few heartbeats later, a second scream sounded.

This time they knew exactly where the sound came from: the middle of the slavers' camp. Without much consideration, both men crawled as close as possible without the Varas seeing them. But once they peered through the grasses, they knew they needn't worry. The guards were focused on the spectacle a few steps from them.

The entry to the captain's tent exploded outward, and Terja glanced at Joven in shock. They'd both thought the person being tortured would be one of the captives, but it wasn't. Xain stumbled away from the tent with his arms and torso covered with lash marks. With each crack of Geir's whip, another soul-shriveling scream erupted from Xain's throat.

"Filthy Talac! You do not touch your better. You know this." Geir lashed him again.

"Please, Master. Please, I will not fail you again."

Geir flipped the whip in his hand and drove the thick handle into Xain's stomach. He dropped to the ground gasping for air.

"Get up, you worthless animal!" Geir's whip snaked out again and left a crimson stripe down Xain's back. He looked at the pitifully whimpering man lying before him. Even from a distance, Terja and Joven could hear everything. "Get him out of my sight. Throw him out of the barrier. Let the animals that so easily kill my men pick over his bones."

Two of the burly guards grabbed Xain and carried him into the forest. The remaining people resumed their duties acting as if nothing had happened. The captives were completely cowed, except the golden one. The sun touched the trees on the western horizon before the two guards returned.

They watched the camp to see if there were clues that this was a trap. But it appeared the traitor had been killed and the body discarded. Terja motioned to Joven, and they moved from their observation spot. Once they were far enough away, Terja leaned closer and whispered, "We need to get back to camp and tell Anan what happened."

ANAN SQUATTED on his heels and stared into the forest surrounding them.

"Where did you find the body?" Anan asked.

Terja jerked his head toward the sun. "A short walk that direction. Quite a distance from their camp."

"But much closer to ours."

Terja nodded.

"They killed the one person who made it possible to attack the clans."

"Yes. Perhaps he couldn't do it anymore. Joven said he was taking matama from their kilts. They must all be empty now."

"Maybe. He was beaten? By the captain?"

"Yes, and we could see the wounds appear and bleed."

"They couldn't know we were there," said Joven. "It doesn't make sense to set up something for us. And what're the chances of stumbling over his body? None. But it's Xain's fault the Varas killed so many. Why should we save him?"

Anan considered for a moment before making his decision. "We don't know why. Perhaps there's a reason. We don't even know where the matama came from for the first village they attacked. And he's Talac. We could at least perform his unraveling."

He handed his bow and quiver to Joven and then looked at them both. "If something happens, fill him with arrows. We can't let him get to the Varas with more information." He fixed his gaze on Terja. "Take him if you can. You're formidable with your sling."

Terja swallowed hard. "Yes, we'll make sure he doesn't get back."

"Stay here, and be prepared."

Anan covered the distance to the unmoving body. Once he arrived, he circled twice, looking once with his eyes and once with weaver's vision. Neither showed more than he expected. Even the man's kilt was different, made from plants and creating a sensation slightly different than kuri fabric. Every fiber in his being resonated with the wrongness of it all. But he couldn't think of a reason to not at least see if he were alive. He reached out and remembered the body itself could be a trap. Stepping back for a third check, he ran his vision over the ground he rested on and found nothing.

126

Anan glanced up to see the other pair moving closer but motioned them away. "No, keep your distance." He considered for a moment. "Stay apart."

He waited until they completed his instructions, then turned back to the body. He lowered himself and then reached out, braced to whatever he might find. When his finger touched Xain's shoulder, it was still warm and pliant. His vision dropped into place, and he saw the body and the damage. Old scars crisscrossed Xain, and most were impossible to see without a weaver's vision. But Anan could tell the injuries were genuine. Breath and blood still flowed. He was alive.

Anan laid his hand across Xain's chest and wove a small spell. He wasn't willing to use more than a tiny amount of weaving to close off some of the bleeding. Distantly he noted the blood loss didn't seem serious, but the thought was lost with Anan's initial touch.

He worked selectively, repairing where the blood flowed more heavily. As he worked, he realized the man was conscious. Anan stepped out of reach. "I know you're awake."

The eyes slowly opened until they stared at each other. "My name is Xain. I was not certain what response I would get from a fellow Talac."

Anan rested his hand on his warrior sword. As he watched, the man slowly moved until he was seated. He dusted his hands and grimaced when he moved. "As a weaver I had thought you might share your name."

Anan studied him for a few moments, then answered. "I am Anan. Come on. I'll help you." He extended his hand and helped Xain to his feet. Anan let him stand and sway for several breaths until he was able to walk. He motioned Xain ahead of him, keeping a hand on his weapon.

He heard the others converging on them and opened his vision to see if any of the Varas followed them. He could only detect the four of them, and Joven no longer moved to join with them. He drifted slowly away, taking Anan's bow and quiver of arrows with him. Anan's weaving tracked him for a short time, but Joven was leaving.

Cursing his misjudgment under his breath, he saw Xain stop. "Focus ahead. I'd hate to have to kill you after I closed your wounds."

Xain looked ahead, and they moved only a few steps before Terja appeared from the brush and walked beside him. He caught Anan's glance and motioned his head in the direction Joven went. "You saw?"

Anan nodded and then motioned his chin ahead of them "Yes. It can be dealt with later."

Terja gave him a long look, then focused on Xain. They worked their way from the meadow, but the sense of unease did not leave Anan. Xain never made an extra move, but Anan still found himself waiting for any excuse to kill the traitor. They approached the camp he and Joven set for tonight, but the feeling of wrongness continued to grow, like a poorly woven fabric, full of mistakes and holes.

They moved into the sheltered area, and Xain looked around. "Where are the others? There must be others. It would take more than the two of you to kill off Geir's men."

Terja met Anan's eyes and then looked back. "There are no others."

Xain studied the surrounding area as both men watched him. His legs suddenly gave out, and he dropped to the ground. He made a flurry of motions with his hands and released a weaving hidden in the fabric of his kilt.

"Kill him! He's weaving." Before Anan could respond, the world went black.

CHAPTER THIRTEEN

PAIN WASHED over Anan, as if he were filled with a multitude of thorns. The snap of canvas and the vile odor washing across the floor where his cheek rested told him he was living his worst fear.

"Oh, good. They're beginning to awaken."

Anan lunged upward, and the metal rings around his neck and wrists snapped tight as he reached the end of the chain tethering him to a massive center pole. His vision blurred as he strained against the anchor, and he could see almost nothing. As the numbness oozed into his limbs, the pain of injuries rushed in to fill his body. He fought to see the man squatting just out of reach as his head jerked backward.

"Excellent, Xain. Of course, the big one will pay for killing my men. But I know a particularly nasty sex pit owner who will teach him obedience," Geir said, devoid of emotion.

Anan heard the voice that would echo through his mind for as long as he lived. A Talac face swam before him. He looked into the traitor's eyes and saw delight.

"How are you, weaver?"

Anan swallowed hard as a wave of nausea flowed through his body. He rolled and retched, emptying whatever might have been in his stomach, then flopped to his back. He shot Xain a hate-filled glance. "By the Twined Ones, you will pay for this, Xain."

Anan's head snapped around when Xain's fist slammed into his jaw. "Silence, slave. The Varas know of many ways to make death seem preferable without leaving a mark."

Anan struggled to contain his bile. When a familiar body hit the ground beside him, his own suffering had no meaning. Blood from a fingercount of wounds covered Terja. Anan's horror deepened when he realized he could no longer sense Terja through their connection. A choking gasp rolled from Anan's lips as he found more injuries. "Terja, wake up!"

The only response was silence.

"Poor spinner. It's too bad the Varas didn't know what they had until I told them. They thought your little partner was a Varas traitor, and they have a strange habit of beheading traitors. No Varas ever captured a spinner before, you know. They have such a bad habit of killing themselves and any Varas around them." He studied Terja for a moment. "Although it did give me some retribution for the lash marks I got to set the trap for you two. We chose this spot to give you a good place to watch the performance. I'm glad you didn't miss it."

Geir motioned the guards out. "Leave us."

The burly men exited the tent, leaving only him, Geir, Xain, and a still unconscious Terja. He turned to the pair, anger filling him. His vision slid into place, and he reached for his kilt and the weavings he and Terja had so carefully created, to find nothing. Their kilts were as white as the day they left the looms. All their hard work filling the spell panels was gone. He glared at the traitor with hate-filled eyes. "How did you take it? I never gave you permission and I am no weak underfed captive. You can't use my weavings unless I let you."

Xain stood silently until the tent flaps were secured and the sound of footsteps could no longer be heard. Then he stepped into the light and smiled at Anan in a way he hoped to never see again. "That was the only useful thing I got from my parents. I am no spinner, but I can weave from anyone's work without permission. It has kept me alive since before I was sold to the Varas. You had more war colors stored than I've ever seen. You have an impressive little spinner." He gestured toward Terja. "Your connection also made the task of capturing you much easier than I'd thought. One little yank, and you were both out cold."

Xain studied the unconscious spinner for a few moments before turning to him. "He's quite valuable, you know. They won't even put him in a house of pleasure—if he cooperates."

"Terja would never help you. He would never desert his people."

Xain turned on him, his face contorted with rage. "My honorable Talac parents sold me to the Varas. Geir bought me and nursed me back to health. Where would your allegiance be?"

Xain walked around him as he might a prized kuri sire. Anan braced himself, refusing to let the examination unnerve him. Xain completed his inspection before returning to stand beside Geir. "Oh, I believe he will do whatever we tell him to keep his twining alive." He turned to speak with Geir, his voice quivering with excitement. "It is a spellspinner. He is exactly as described, no patterned velvet. Almost a taller version of you Varas, without the dense beards."

Geir's gaze shifted to Xain. "Then he can heal my children."

Xain nodded, his expression becoming feral. "He will, or we can slice on his precious twining until he does."

Anan swallowed hard, shocked Xain could sense their tie. He started to speak, but Xain motioned him into silence. "Save your words, weaver. I'm capable of seeing a twining bond." He looked at Anan for a moment, then continued. "Granted, yours will be somewhat more difficult to manipulate, but then, I've never seen a pairing thread with a spinner." He licked his lips in a way that made Anan consider deathspinners harmless pets.

His resolve hardened, and his eyes narrowed as he focused on Xain. "How could you do this? You've wiped out at least two full clans. Those who still live will know only a weaver could take down the village webs. Why? Why would you do this to your own people?"

He smirked before he grasped Geir and kissed the Varas hard. They continued for several breaths before separating with a gasp. Anan watched in shock as he pushed Geir downward until he knelt in front of the Talac. He pressed the Varas's face into his crotch, forcing him against his hardening cock as Geir started to chew along its length. Xain raked his eyes over Anan as he began slamming his groin against Geir's face.

He split his attention between Geir and Anan. Xain pistoned his hips again and again against the Varas as an evil smile filled his lips. "The weaver's velvet is addictive to some Varas, particularly those who are descendants of the House of the Sun." He reached down to run his fingers across the pale hair on Geir's head. After pulling Geir's head back, Xain spat in his face and then kissed him hard.

"He will do whatever I ask of him to feed his addiction. Anything. And he knows I am the one who can best satiate his needs." He glared at Anan. "I won't be in someone else's power again. No one else will discard me like my worthless Talac parents. Now I have the power over Geir. And your little twining will cure his family, or you will discover why the Red Gods are so bloodthirsty."

Anan tried to turn away but found weavings in place that left him frozen. Xain focused on him and shook his head. "My weaves are good. I've tricked other Talac slaves to share their spells before they died. The freeze weavings of the Meke clan were easily learned when she thought I had a way to escape. She escaped like all slaves. Her body was fed to the great river serpents."

Forced to watch the two, Anan's disgust grew as evidence of Geir's addiction mounted. He clawed at the lacings on Xain's kilt, ripping it open. As the garment fell to the ground, Geir rubbed his face against Xain's velvet, his expression a study in bliss. Xain wrapped his hand around his hard cock and slapped it across the slaver's face. In a few heartbeats, strands of his essence covered Geir. He opened his mouth when Xain rubbed himself over his lips, letting him slip deep into his throat.

Anan was forced to see the two participate in a subversion of intimacy. The only threads surrounding the pair were lust and depravity. For Anan, their actions were a travesty of twining. This was a perversion of the gift of the Twined Ones.

As Geir took the last of Xain's hard cock, he closed his eyes and moaned. Xain's focus returned to Anan. "You see, this entire expedition is my idea. The lure of capturing a Talac spellspinner to cure his family simply made it all the easier. Geir doesn't have the intelligence to plan something like this. He is a slave to my body and knows how best to pleasure me. And to sweeten the treat, withdrawal from his addiction is usually fatal."

He pinned Geir's head between his hands and thrust hard, causing him to gag. Then he continued. "They get the addiction for Talac in the pleasure houses. We are very popular. Some believe the cured pelts are the equal of a living Talac." He grabbed Geir's chin and forced him to meet his gaze. "Isn't that right, lover? You considered the stories of using pelts in your bedroom, but you knew they wouldn't be enough, even if the tales were true."

Geir trembled in his grasp, but the moment he released him, he rubbed his face over Xain's body with soft mewing sounds.

"I might have never seen a spinner before, but I know how love twists people. Your twining will heal Geir's family. Because otherwise, we will carve you into pieces in a way that will make the deathspinners seem humane," Xain said.

What? Even if he has never seen a spinner, how can Xain not know weavers are the healers?

Xain's smile contained no indication of compassion. "The broken Talac are sent to the pits, and not much is left by the time they die there. But with your little healer, the Talac will last longer. Geir will become more wealthy and powerful. Someday, with me behind him, he will be High Regency."

He shifted his focus, slamming his hard cock into Geir's mouth again and again. His breath came in gasps as he neared orgasm. Anan could never imagine shared intimacy being so repulsive. Xain groaned, and his orgasm began, a white stream leaking from the corner of Geir's mouth. Anan tasted bile as Xain's body shook. Time seemed to stretch out forever as he was forced to watch.

Xain pulled out of his mouth and wiped his dripping cock over Geir's face while he struggled to get each drop. He smiled languidly at Anan while Geir nursed the last drops from his softening shaft. "See how easy they are to satisfy, Anan? Perhaps you can find a patron in the pleasure house. One that likes his Talac meaty and rough." He strode across the room until he was a finger length from Anan.

"Now understand, Kuri. I am in charge. Geir will do as I tell him because otherwise he will suffer an addict's death that makes that granted by the deathspinners merciful. And if you cause me trouble, you will suffer, but nothing in comparison to the punishment your little spinner will get. Yes, your lover will suffer, but I won't allow him to die. Just suffer, forever."

Anan's body locked in a haze of fury. *This one will pay.*

The fog of anger thinned when he realized Xain was still talking. "The Varas are masters of torture. I'm sure you will meet Kotu soon and learn the extent of their skills. But he won't kill you. He knows Geir will do worse than kill him if he did. Oh yes, the rest of the trip should be entertaining."

Xain's gaze flipped around the room as a froth formed at the corners of his mouth. Anan realized the traitor's mind was gone. Geir stood, appearing to have regained some level of sanity. But Anan saw the front of his pants were wet from his orgasm. He met Geir's gaze without flinching.

"Take your little spinner and join the other slaves. Just remember what I've said," Xain said.

Released, Anan turned without a word, lifted Terja in his arms, and started toward the opening. He glanced back to see Xain helping Geir clean himself. The entire scene replayed for Anan, and his revulsion grew. He turned away from them and scratched on the tent covering. It was opened in an instant and then sealed behind them.

Anan was led through the camp to the slave lines, treating the four guards who surrounded them with the disdain of royalty for bodyguards.

He stumbled and almost fell when Terja whispered, "I heard. Be strong."

SONERI WATCHED from the corner of his eye as the large weaver walked toward the slave lines. He'd been shocked at first to realize he was carrying a spinner, a very alive spinner. He couldn't imagine the circumstances that might cause a spellspinner to be captured.

Even in his small group, when they were attacked their spinner drained two of the Varas before the akhir killed him. But Soneri had learned one thing in the days since his capture: this was not a normal Varas slave raid.

The two drew closer, and one of the guards drew back the haft of his spear. The weaver glared at the guard, and Soneri could almost sense the command. The Varas hesitated, then stepped into formation around the two of them. They brought them to the same section of bindings as Soneri and Morea, hammering their restraints into the links of the slave chains.

He kept his distance as the weaver lowered the spinner to the ground, leaning him against a tree. Soneri moved closer, feeling the need to help. After a few moments, the weaver turned to him. "Water."

Soneri retrieved the waterskin without questioning and handed it over. The water was dripped into the spinner's mouth. The spinner swallowed, and Soneri realized he was conscious. He shifted his body to block the guard's view as Morea did the same on the opposite side. They watched through veiled lashes as drop by drop the water passed over the spinner's cracked lips. The drips continued until he opened his eyes. His gaze went from Soneri to Morea, and a nod passed to the weaver.

The weaver spoke in a voice barely loud enough to be heard. "My name is Anan; this is Terja. We are of the Kuri clan. We've been following the slavers for most of a moon. They wiped out most of our clan, and we found them only a handful of days ago." He paused significantly. "The Twined Ones have blessed our bloodweaving."

Soneri replied in an equally low voice. "I am Soneri, and this is Morea, who is also Kuri. I am the only survivor from the attack on my group. We were few, only family members. The Varas hunted our clan even before this, so our numbers were not great." Anan locked eyes with Soneri, then nodded.

"So you're responsible for the death among the Varas?" Soneri asked.

Terja smiled as he pushed himself upward and met Soneri's gaze. "I believe the Varas were clumsy, and the hazards of the Talac's land overcame them."

Soneri glanced at the closest guard. "Yes, the Talac do not live in a land that tolerates fools or mistakes. The combination of both is fatal."

They spent the remainder of the night asking questions about the slavers. Anan and Terja were happy to be told the Varas were down to slightly more than a double fingercount of men. Which also meant they took no chances now; even Morea was tied to the chains and not released. Tensions were high, and the capture of Terja strained the nerves of the Varas even further. They'd never seen a living spinner, but everyone knew they were the source of the Talac's akhir magic, though they were not sure how.

Soneri waited until everyone but a few night guards were asleep, and moved to hide what was being done. Terja had harvested matama and created the threads that Anan used to fill their kilt panels, keeping the most useful for the task ahead of them. Most of the spellweavers could make small changes in the Varas metals, the best being able to unweave them.

Soneri was amazed to discover that Anan believed he could do it. His shock deepened when he realized Terja was feeding Anan matama directly along their mating-bond. But his attention shifted back to find Anan focused over the chains that linked them all together. Soneri could sense the tremendous flow of matama between them.

"Stop, stop. Or we'll save them the trouble of killing us," whispered Terja urgently.

Anan dropped his hands, the cuffs making a slight chime that attracted the attention of a guard. Anan was drenched in sweat with a slight tremor traveling through his body. The metal had resisted their efforts and left them obviously exhausted. Soneri brought the waterskin, which they drained between the two of them. Anan caught Soneri's gaze and nodded to the cuffs.

Soneri touched the metal and explored the bindings. It took only a few moments before he delivered the news they all dreaded.

"They are pitted and malformed but just as strong as before. Even the lock seems undamaged."

Anan yelped in pain and shock when a lash struck, leaving a bloody track across his shoulder.

"Up, vermin! Today we reach the blessed lands!"

TERJA FELL to the ground, unable to take another step, when the march stopped. The physical toll was tremendous, his body a mesh of lash marks. The slavers had no reason to take care with the whip on him. Geir's threat of dismemberment for anyone who killed him kept the attacks from becoming fatal. But they knew he and Anan were responsible for the deaths of the other Varas. Anan had fared worse.

The swaying figure of Anan stood over him, his legs and buttocks covered in rivulets of blood. Xain had been right about one thing: the Varas were experts at inflicting pain. They demonstrated their knowledge today with great skill. The one they called Kotu showed his particular delight in the damage he could inflict by tying a few shards of metal to the end of his whip.

Anan was depleted from the weavings of the night before. While Terja gathered threads all day, he had little hope of being able to try again. The pressured march of the day coupled with Anan's blood loss…. Terja wondered if they knew how close they were to losing their pet spinner. If Anan died, Terja had no reason to withhold akhir, and he planned to take as many Varas with him as possible.

Like a carrion fly to rotting flesh, Geir appeared, with Xain close behind. Geir looked at Anan, and then his gaze shifted to Terja. "I will make this clear. If you try your little spinner trick, not only will I gut your lover." He motioned to Soneri and Morea. "I will kill the yellow one and the female too. Very. Slowly." Then his gaze shifted to Anan. "Tomorrow we will be in Varas territory, and we will begin your training for the pleasure houses."

A shiver of horror slipped through Terja. How many lives was it worth? Talon-like fingers grabbed his jaw and tilted it upward until Xain's face filled his vision. "Don't try akhir, or we will wipe your friends from the face of existence. And we will burn the bodies so they can't rejoin the Great Weaving."

Terja struggled to find his connection to Anan again but located only a trickle of pain and despair, and he didn't need their twining connection to sense that. He knew the time would come for his akhir. And when it did, Xain would be his first target. And if it meant the death of everyone, including Anan, then he would be judged for his actions by First Spinner. But he knew he had to stop the Varas from doing this again.

The rest of Xain's threats were wasted on Terja; he was already gathering the strength he would need in order to drain at least Geir and Xain before the backlash destroyed him. This time he could expect no rescue from Anan.

By the time the blackness of night cycled to the gray of predawn, he and Anan were prepared. Terja moved until they were touching.

"Our time together has been good. I have no regret for having twined with you," Anan said.

"If you two would be still, it'd be helpful" came a whispered demand.

Terja froze, recognizing the voice. "Joven, what are you doing?"

"I'm here to get you out. What do you think I'm doing?"

"You left," Terja said, "When we were taking Xain to camp."

Joven shook his head. "Something was wrong. It felt off since we'd watched Geir beat Xain. Then I realized, the barrier never wavered while Xain was taken from their camp, and he was the only one to create it. But I couldn't remember if it had been still in place when we left. So I moved away to keep Xain from knowing I was there." Joven frowned. "After he knocked you out, Varas swarmed you. I just hoped I'd find a way to get you out of here."

Joven studied the iron restraints for a moment before turning to Terja. "I found the silk after the Varas left. Spin it with whatever matama you've harvested."

Not certain what the young man had planned, Terja resisted the demand until Joven jerked at his collar. "Make the threads if you want to escape. At least I can try to unweave the iron."

Terja grabbed the handful of silk Joven held and began spinning it with the matama. It flooded across the deathspinner fiber, a multicolored swirl of threads that had no pattern or order. But Joven grabbed the spinning and began his weaving. Terja's spinner's vision slipped into place, allowing him to follow Joven's weaving. The threads disappeared into the chains but did nothing more than Anan accomplished the previous night. The warp of the weaving tightened and broke one by one until it was obvious Joven's spell was no more effective.

"Hey! What are you doing?"

Soneri moved to hide Joven as the guard walked toward them with his whip uncurled. "I said what's going on?"

Anan turned to him. "Praying to the Twined Ones that the Varas are all dead soon."

The whip he held snapped to life around Anan's throat and yanked them together. He twisted the braided leather of the whip even tighter. "They won't find your body until morning...." Anan struggled to breathe, his efforts becoming more and more frantic.

Suddenly the Varas lunged to his toes. Soneri covered his mouth and grabbed the back of his head. With a twist of his hands and a crack of bones, he broke the man's neck. He held the flailing body until it quieted and then dropped it to the ground.

Terja knotted his brows as he tried to work out how they could possibly survive. The death of the guard would be discovered as soon as he didn't check in with the next sentry in the chain. If that happened before they were gone, their chances of surviving became almost none. One of the moons flickered through the clouds, and he saw the others watching him. *Oh, ravelings. When did I become the leader?* He considered the failure of both Anan and Joven to try to unweave their irons.

He lifted Anan's neckring and studied the iron band with its intricate lock. With a second exploration through his sight, he couldn't help but feel it looked similar. Not quite a weaving, but something close.

"What are you looking for? We've already tried. None of us have the skill to unweave it, and Geir keeps the keys," Anan said.

"It looks familiar. Like a pattern I should know."

"What? I've looked at the lock. The only thing I've seen as complicated were the Twined One's sandals."

Terja's head snapped up, and determination filled him. "That's it. That's the pattern." He spun on Anan. "You can unweave the locks. The Paired Ones gave us the pattern already."

The others watched quietly as Anan stared at the dark iron in his hands. Terja hoped that now that Anan knew where he'd seen the pattern of knots and ties before. As he worked, Terja searched through the information he'd gotten from the teaching weavings. He grabbed Anan's shoulder, demanding attention.

"These are from Ubica smiths. There is something like matama beaten into the iron. Look at the lattice. I think you can slip the lattice that joins them." He inhaled slowly. "Be careful. The Ubica...."

Anan returned the affectionate gesture. "I know about the assassin people. But this isn't one of their traps. That would take a Ubica to arm."

Sweat matted Anan's velvet as he struggled to open the locks. He tugged at the ring again, still to no avail.

"Try our twining connection."

There was a moment of hesitation before Terja felt the tug that was becoming familiar. Matama flooded from Terja, and he caught the quick smile of success Anan shot to him. He pulled any matama he could sense and sent it through their connection to Anan. He could tell Anan was making progress, but then an audible click sounded, and the ring around Anan's neck slipped free.

Anan removed each of the rings keeping him captive and then turned to Terja. In a fingercount of heartbeats, he'd freed Terja also. Their eyes met as the swirl of shared relief filled them. He turned to Terja.

"Who else? They're going to realize the sentry is gone soon."

Terja pointed to Morea and Soneri. "Release those two, or the Varas will kill them. Even Soneri's velvet wouldn't buy him mercy after killing the guard and helping us escape."

Anan focused briefly and Terja heard the soft clicks as the locks opened. Anan began to move, but Terja could sense the pain and exhaustion feeding along their connection. Each step was a painful burden. Anan motioned the others ahead of him. "Go. Leave me the knife, Joven. I'll make them pay for attacking the Talac."

Terja was surprised at the expression of fierce determination on Joven's face when he spun back to them. "No. I won't leave you here. The others can go, but I'm not."

"I had no intentions of leaving him. But he needs to be healed. Use the matama still in your kilt and scorch the lash marks closed."

Joven stared at Terja and then Anan before he shrugged. "Brace yourself. I'm still wearing the war kilt, and it's mostly red matama. This is going to hurt."

Anan clenched his teeth as the wounds were cauterized. Terja could smell the burning flesh as the spell cleaned the wounds of infection and seared the weeping lash marks closed. He knew the weaving was painful beyond belief, but the only response from Anan was a tightening of his muscles. As Anan began to relax, there was a touch at Terja's shoulder.

He spun, not knowing what to expect. Hands grabbed his wrists, and there was a hoarse whisper. "It's Soneri. I can help."

Terja paused, then relaxed. He turned to see Anan struggling against the pain to sit, but with his old look of determination. Soneri motioned them ahead, lifted Anan to his shoulder, and trotted to follow. As they passed from the slave pens, Joven ducked into a small thicket and reemerged again almost immediately. He passed Terja his staff and shield and held up Anan's bow.

"I thought you might want these back. The Varas weren't doing a very good job of taking care of them."

Terja nodded, enjoying the feel of the heavy wood under his touch. "Thank you, Joven. You are the hero tonight."

They returned to the path away from the camp as the Varas camp exploded with shouts and curses. Terja motioned them frantically ahead of him. "Hurry. They've found the guard."

He struggled to keep moving, the stress of the night becoming overwhelming. A protective weaving surged over him, and he almost wept with relief. The others knew it happened, too, and came to a stop. After a short rest, they made slow progress in the direction Terja sent the others. As they moved farther from the Varas camp, the weaving shrunk behind them, snapping from tree to tree. Joven wondered who was controlling it.

They arrived at a dark clearing and found Morea standing in the center of a maelstrom of spell energy, her hair moving as if the strands were alive. She had sprinted ahead of them and woven a protective web faster than Terja would have thought possible.

Her kilt was empty! How can she spin matama?

He reached out and touched her. "How are you...."

Her eyes sprung open, and she unclenched a fist from around a dark red strip. Joven must have handed her a filled spell panel. Ignoring everyone else, she swept the group for Joven and threw herself at him. Her arms wrapped around him tightly enough that he gasped for air. A few moments later she released Joven and whispered, "I thought you were dead. We all thought you were. What happened?"

Terja stepped between the two friends. "That's a long story for when we have more time. Right now we need to get farther away from the Varas." Anan stepped beside him, leaning heavily against Soneri. He looked at his twining. "How far can you travel?"

"Until I drop."

Terja nodded grimly. "So as far as any of us."

Moving as fast as possible, they traveled farther and farther into the dense forest. Although they had traveled many lengths, they still heard an angry din from the direction of the Varas. Joven paused for a moment before turning back. "Not much longer. I found a hiding place close to here."

CHAPTER FOURTEEN

XAIN STOOD with his arms folded, his naked body tense as he recalled the disastrous events of the past day. He wasn't certain if the camp was still being watched or not. *If it were me, I'd be halfway across the grasslands by now, but these Kuri seemed to have an obsession with being heroes.* Xain would have happily given them a path to take, straight to the River of the Burning Twins. He hoped they were foolish enough to return. This time he didn't care how much profit was wasted. Both of them would die horribly.

"Come, Xain. They will not escape us. Kotu is tracking them."

His demeanor shifted into seduction before he gazed at Geir. "Of course we will. They are just primitive Talac. They're lucky the Red Gods let them breathe the same air as the Varas. Even the Forever Words say they are to be slaves to the Varas."

Geir motioned to the sleeping platform beside him. "Come, we can enjoy each other again. My hunger grows with each touch of your hands."

Xain slithered beside Geir, pushing him onto his back. He drifted into the familiar movements he had learned so well during his time at the pleasure house. In an instant, Geir was again in his power. His sight dropped into place, and Xain took a few threads of the matama still remaining on the captives' kilts. Down to the final bits, he rationed each fragment against a time of urgent need. But after the four captives escaped, his hold on Geir had slipped. He had to make certain Geir was still under his control. He pulled the thread to him and, with a few finger motions, wove the spell. A final gesture released the energy. As the magic threaded its way through Geir's body, Xain responded automatically and released his mind to scheme his next move.

143

Guards had discovered the missing slaves before dawn, about the same time a sentry was found with his neck broken. In Geir's fury, he'd almost killed the man who told him, as well as Xain. Once he'd calmed enough to allow Xain to leave his sight, Xain had examined the neck rings and cuff and found every lock open. They'd opened Ubica locks?

He wasn't sure how they'd gotten the big weaver out of camp without drawing attention to themselves. Xain had checked on them last night and didn't think the weaver would survive another day. The guards had taken delight in flaying his legs with their whips to the point that he could barely walk. But somehow they'd managed to not only escape, but take one of the females, as well as Geir's precious golden-pelted Talac. The cascade of problems had caused Xain's influence to lessen.

He refocused on pleasuring Geir, grinding his pelvis against him, and worked harder at giving him pleasure than he had in moons. He twisted and turned to give Geir as much contact with his velvet as possible. His addiction was real, he needed Xain to survive. But even then, the strength of Xain's position was questionable.

He pressed harder and let Geir's cock skid over his abdomen until the captain shook in his arms. His climax shot between them, and as every other time, he suppressed his revulsion. Once the jerky movements of his orgasm ended, he lay across Geir's body. He stayed with Geir until he drifted off to sleep, then untangled them from each other and dressed.

He laced his kilt shut and carefully peered out the tent flap to check the area. After finding it deserted, he stepped into the afternoon light. He studied the camp for a moment, checking the new weaving that was keyed to alert him if it were tampered with. He'd underestimated the escapees. They had unraveled the intruder web last night. He had made the same mistake as the clans, and he wanted to take out his anger on someone, or something. His path led him to the captives, and he ran his tongue over his lips in anticipation.

"You don't get to play with them either."

He jumped, startled by Kotu. "I thought you were tracking the escaped slaves."

"We found traces close to camp. They will be back in irons by tomorrow, or there will be fresh pelts." He motioned toward the slave pens. "I've lost two of the captives I'd singled out for—special attention. Unless you want to stand in for them, stay away from the slaves."

The thought of Kotu's idea of excitement made his blood run cold. While he'd served in the pleasure houses, he'd seen what men like Kotu did to bring themselves to orgasm. The pain of others heightened the intensity of their lust. The worst of them would torture their victims for cycles before finally killing them. Once a slave had received the mark of one of the masters of horror, they knew they would be in the pits soon, if they survived at all.

Kotu would happily carve pieces of flesh from his body while raping him. He'd looked at the monster, using his vision only once. Never before had he seen such a twisted and broken weaving in someone who still lived.

Rather than trying to deal with Kotu, he slipped past him with a look of fury at the bound slaves. He grabbed a crossbow from one of the guards, who stepped away. Xain moved into the forest and paused. Rounding on the guard he'd just disarmed, he snarled, "Well? Are you coming? Geir wants fresh meat for tonight."

SONERI STUDIED each of the other people in the camp. This group was almost as large as his home clan. Well, perhaps not as large, but his home clan was tiny compared to the Kuri. He had been the only one with a sun-touched velvet, though. He had always been told that his coloration made him a target, a trophy some people would do anything, pay anything, to attain.

Now, he'd been given a new life. He knew Joven only from the few days they were in captivity together and the other two not at all. Yet they had saved him. He turned to Anan and started to explain. "I have to go. They'll never leave you alone as long as I'm here. My skin is too valuable."

"No," said Anan.

"No? What do you—"

"No," echoed Terja. "We are all together, and we are going to rescue the others."

"But you could leave. They wouldn't follow you back into Kuri territory. Especially if they knew I wasn't with you."

Morea walked to Soneri, motioned him closer, and cupped his face in her small hands. "We are not sacrificing you. We need you to help save everyone."

He looked from face to face, seeing similar denial of any chance they would use him as a bargaining chit. From Joven he got an impression of more, of some tenuous connection. The look concerned him, uncertain of its source. With a slight hesitation, he nodded his acceptance of their unspoken promise.

Anan used what little matama they had to lay a warning thread around them. It would give them a heartbeat of notice if the Varas found them. As he laid the last wisp into place, he glanced toward Terja.

"Xain drained all of our matama panels. That's how they got past the guardian webs."

Terja blushed red and looked away. "There's a way."

"What?" Soneri asked. "If it gives us a chance…."

Terja locked his eyes on Anan. "Corcra."

His eyebrows shot up as he saw Terja's cheeks turn the color of a bloodfruit. Soneri understood exactly what was being asked, and given.

Anan's face was a close match in color when he tried to speak. What came out was almost a squeak. "That wouldn't be enough. Unless we went further."

Soneri looked from one to the other of the men, knowing where this conversation must go. It was their only hope.

Terja locked eyes with Anan, and they stood as unmoving as an ironwood tree. Soneri had no way of telling what they shared through their connection, but only a short time passed before a faint smile came across Terja's lips and he dropped his eyes.

"Maybe," Terja said. "Maybe it will work."

TERJA LAID his shield to one side of the sheltered area they'd found not far from that night's camp. He studied the flora around them as he unlaced his kilt. Once they had made the decision to use corcra again, it had taken only a short time to prepare. With the last bit unlaced, he uncoiled the fabric from his slender hips, folded it, and laid it to one side.

As he moved closer, he lifted Anan's hands away and finished unlacing his kilt. He eased the material over the twin mounds of his butt cheeks and put it with his. He stepped in tight, feeling Anan's heat radiate over him as he ran his hands over the muscular torso. He leaned in closely, kissed his chin, and then leaned back. "I've dreamed of this again. Sometimes when I awaken in your arms, I want to share everything with you." Terja smiled. "But then I don't really know what more to share."

As Anan slid his hands down Terja's back, he groaned, their naked bodies grinding against each other. His cock swelled between them, becoming rock hard. Anan slipped his finger between Terja's cheeks and moved lower until he cupped his balls and squeezed them.

"Ah, strands! Careful. So close."

Terja was shocked when Anan knelt in front of him, kissed his taut stomach, and then licked to the hair surrounding his cock. When Anan blew his hot breath over him, his body seized, and clear gel flowed from his slit. Anan pressed his lips against the head of his cock, his tongue darting out and running through the stream. A heartbeat later, Terja was shaking, and a torrent of soft moans escaped his lips. He grabbed Anan and tried to pull him off. "No. No. No!"

With ecstasy flowing through his body, the first torrents of pleasure surged through Terja. Past the edge, he plunged into a powerful orgasm. Anan gripped his hips tightly as wave after wave washed over him. With a final shot, he caught himself against Anan as his body released him.

"Oh, Paired Ones! I've never. Oh. Strands!"

Anan grinned as he ran his hands over his back. "Good. I was hoping so."

Terja sank to his knees, wrapped his arms around Anan's neck, and pressed their lips together. A tongue darted into his mouth, and he relaxed as their tongues intertwined. Terja's cock began to swell, his desire growing with each touch.

He leaned against Anan as they kissed, pressing him onto the ground. He ran his hands down his twining's rippling body, tracing the patterns he found so alluring. The beautiful velvet sent spikes of fire through Terja's system. He moved lower until he was between the muscular legs and stared at the shaft jutting from Anan's groin.

He wrapped his fist around it and pulled back the skin covering. As he did, the crown slipped into view, and slick liquid coated his hand. He leaned closer and flicked the tip of his tongue over the edge. A groan encouraged him, and he traced the thick vein that ran its way around Anan's cock. By the time he'd followed its path, his hand was coated with the slick gel. He slipped his hands lower and smeared the coating over Anan's balls.

"Oh!"

He burrowed his tongue into the longer hair between Anan's legs, and the tang he found sent a surge of lust that left him wanting more. He drove his tongue harder, flooding his senses with Anan's masculine scent and taste. He kissed the tip of Anan's cock and then pressed his mouth down its thick length. He let the hard shaft slide deeper into his throat until it could go no farther. He paused for a moment, relaxed, and the last of the shaft slid between his lips.

"Paired Ones! No one ever did that. Strands! Terja."

Terja quivered with excitement at the response. He gripped his hands over the hard spheres of Anan's butt, surprised to feel the weaver trembling under his touch. He swallowed, and Anan's cock flexed in his mouth. A moment later, he slid his head backward until the shaft twisted loose and slapped against Anan's flat stomach.

Terja glanced up, filled with uncertainty. "Is it... adequate?"

Anan chuckled, then leaned down and kissed Terja, running his hands over his smooth face. "So very far from adequate. A little more, and I'll be filling your mouth."

He grinned, almost bashful, then pried Anan's cock away from his stomach and sucked it between his lips. He began sliding his head up and down the length of Anan's cock as the moans gained in volume and his body shook even harder. Suddenly Anan tensed, and for a heartbeat Terja thought something was wrong, but then the first blast of Anan's come hit against the back of his throat. He swallowed quickly and then struggled as jet after jet shot from Anan. But the tremors slowed, and Terja let the shaft slip out slowly until his lips were pressed against the tip of Anan's cock, and he nursed the last drops. Anan clamped his hands around his head and pulled him off.

"That's enough, or you'll have me squealing like a dying springtail."

Anan cupped Terja's face and pulled him into a soft kiss. "That was like nothing I've felt before. I thought I was going to die from built-up pleasure."

Terja ducked his head as a flash of heat traveled across his face. He gasped at the sensation of Anan's hand wrapping around his cock, which had sprung back to life.

"I think you're ready to go again. What do you think?"

Terja swallowed hard and nodded, unable to focus beyond the ecstasy burning through every fiber of his being. He could feel a second orgasm approaching with each thrust of Anan's hand, but then he stopped.

Terja dropped to sit on his heels, his breath coming in gasps as he teetered on the brink. "What? Why?"

"I think this will fill our silk with corcra," Anan said with a smirk. Before Terja could question him, Anan rolled to his back and pulled his knees to his chest. Terja could only stare at the dusky opening. His cock jerked at the sight. He glanced at Anan, wanting to know the offering was what he thought.

"Go slow. It's been a while."

Terja crawled between Anan's legs and pressed the head of his cock against his opening. Sliding over Anan's velvet was almost his undoing. It felt as if a summer of lightning storms hit at once, and their fire filled Terja with a desire he'd never experienced before. This time it was his body trembling as he eagerly tried to find Anan's opening. He knew this was not simple making of corcra for spells. This formed a knot in his gut when he thought of Anan.

His search became more urgent as the heat of his passion burned like a grasslands fire. Then his cock sank into Anan with no effort. A groan burst from both of them as he drove himself inside Anan. He pressed deeper until his crotch hairs ground against Anan's ass.

"By the Twined Ones! Do it. Harder."

Terja needed little encouragement as his instincts took over and he mated with Anan. He began to sweat as the feelings he thought could get no better, intensified. The slap of his hips against Anan's hard ass, the tight heat around his cock, the burn of sexual euphoria from each place Anan's velvet touched his own smooth skin…. It quickly became too much.

He rose on his toes and slammed into Anan a final time and then emptied himself again into his lover. His body shook with each wave of ecstasy while Anan ran his hands over him in firm caresses. A few heartbeats later, his muscles released, and he collapsed on top of Anan.

"So. So good," he said as he gasped for air.

They lay intertwined until his breathing slowed, and then he looked down at Anan with a grin. "I want that too."

Anan looked concerned. "You sure? I'm thicker than you are."

"But not longer."

A deep chuckle rolled from Anan. "True, but length isn't usually a problem. I have an idea that might help."

Terja eagerly allowed himself to be moved until he was seated over Anan's face. When the weaver's thick hands lowered him, a gasp of pleasure escaped as Anan flicked his tongue over his opening. After a few moments, Terja lost himself again, and the swirl of mating fever surrounded him. It built as Anan's tongue plunged deeper and deeper into his butt. The pleasure grew until he almost screamed when Anan stopped.

"Don't stop! So good."

"This will be even better. You have me so worked up that I am leaking almost as much as you did. I'll go slow, but I think you're ready."

Anan helped Terja lower himself to the ground and then moved behind him. He rubbed his cock up and down Terja's cleft, leaving behind a slick coating. He began to press inward. Terja could feel hard cock against his opening and panted in anticipation. This was unfamiliar territory, and Anan seemed less confident than usual. But the heat between the two of them was not to be denied. His opening was slick and relaxed from Anan's tongue as he felt himself stretch open. The combination of pain and pleasure brought new levels of euphoria through his body. Suddenly Anan slipped through, and Terja groaned as fire and ice ran through him.

He bit down on his lip to keep in a moan that would have alerted any Varas within a half day's journey. Pleasure surged through his body beyond anything he'd ever imagined. When Anan lay across his back, the texture of plush hair was like a million points of ecstasy against him. He arched his back, his mind gone to the aether as the surge of euphoria overcame him.

Feeling like a kuri in mating season, he slammed against Anan with increasing force until he felt the texture of Anan's crotch grind against his butt and the surge of heat almost overcome him. This level of intimacy was far beyond anything he and Anan shared before. The sensations and building lust drove Terja to incoherent hedonism.

Their connection had progressed beyond the physical, and now their emotions wove together like the perfect tapestry of need and want. He felt Anan inside him and sighed when he hit a particularly wonderful spot. Anan pulled out and rammed in again, and he gasped as sparks filled his vision. Terja squirmed and thrashed, wanting more. The bolts of passion that slammed into him again and again had him at the edge.

Anan's breathing was ragged, and his thrusts erratic. He was close to release.

Anan clipped the knot of pleasure deep inside him again, and Terja's eyes rolled back. The ecstasy grew to unbearable levels, and then his body released for an unbelievable third time.

The streams of white littered the ground under them, covering leaves and fabric alike. Terja's flush of elation ran through his body as he trembled uncontrollably under Anan. His body experienced sensations he'd never felt before, but he hoped it wasn't the last time.

As he began to relax, Terja realized Anan had him pinned to the ground. Anan's cock stayed buried deep inside, and he could feel the strong jets filling him. They trembled, their bodies sliding over each other. The spinner stilled and enjoyed the intimacy of their bodies intertwining. The sun had begun its downward arch when Anan began to move and leaned in for a kiss.

"I would guess our efforts were rewarded. Why don't you spin the matama into the silk," Anan said.

Terja nodded, closed his eyes, and blended the silk with their deep purple matama. He opened his eyes—and squeaked. The bundles of fine thread they'd brought were all a solid swirl of the purest color of corcra Terja could imagine. "Twined Ones! We did that?"

Anan chuckled and kissed him again. "I think we were the only ones around."

AS HE and Terja moved closer to their camp, Anan sent out a subtle weaving to check for problems. He found nothing out of the ordinary with the small group. But thought he detected an odd flicker between Soneri and Joven, but when he checked again it was gone.

Regardless of the mysterious threads from the gods, they still had a rescue to plan, and their chances of success were slim. There were still only the five of them, when there were at least twice as many Varas. The slavers who remained were all seasoned veterans. Simple snares and deadfalls would catch none of these men.

But their group—Anan shuddered to realize he was the most experienced of them. As he stood considering his choices, Terja appeared beside him and rested his hand on Anan's shoulder.

"You're planning again. And spending time in wasted worry."

"What am I going to do? A moon ago I was Silbre's mate and spent most of my time hunting. Now I'm supposed to save the Talac. I don't see many ways this ends in success."

Terja squeezed his shoulder. "We harvested deathspinner fiber for new spell panels. Corcra fills many of them. We've saved three captives, and the Twined Ones blessed our bloodweaving."

Anan shook his head. "And what about after? If we do release all the captives? The Kuri are herders, but our herds are gone. We couldn't find them, and Joven remembers nothing. What does that mean?"

"What about the herds?" Joven asked.

They realized Joven and Soneri were close enough to hear them. "We were talking about when we return to the Kuri lands. We need the herds. If they're gone, how will the clan survive? Are any of the animals alive?"

"Yes," Soneri said.

"How do you know? You aren't even Kuri."

"Because the Varas have no kuri pelts and no store of kuri meat. So they didn't slaughter the herds."

Anan considered for a moment, his mouth twisted in a scowl. "And the Iceweaver's season is coming quickly. It might have already started on the grazing lands." Anan could almost feel the bite of cold as he considered their future.

Soneri shrugged. "We'll worry about that once we've survived the rescue. If I go on to the Great Weaving, I won't care about the herds."

Anan stopped himself and shoved the dark thoughts away, knowing they would give their lives to keep the other Talac from becoming the slaves of the Varas. Even with only these few fighters, they would try. They had no choice.

The men made their way to the tiny fire Morea tended in front of their shelter. Anan motioned everyone to gather around a patch of smooth sand. He picked up a stick and quickly sketched out the area around them before he glanced at the other four.

"Tomorrow we will begin our attack. Terja and I confirmed it with the knowledge weavings from the Talac—it's an obsidian sun. We will attack when the twined moons darken the world."

Soneri frowned. "Are you certain?"

Anan crouched lightly on the balls of his feet and looked at the other man. "Terja can read the weavings. I trust Terja." His eyes narrowed as he considered the young man. "It really doesn't matter what the weavings say, we have to try tomorrow. Our chances are almost none as it is, but if we wait that faint hope will be gone when they leave the foothills and enter the Varas's lands."

Anan paused, meeting each person's gaze before he continued. "Terja and I are on a bloodweaving. We'll continue until the captives are free or we are dead. That doesn't have to be the same for you."

Soneri tensed and started to speak, but when he met Anan's determined gaze, he stopped. Time ceased to exist as the two considered each other. The others watched the silent struggle that stretched out until Soneri dropped his gaze. Anan stared after him for several long breaths before resuming.

"All the Varas have extra crossbows. But they've started only loading one at a time so their sinew bowstrings don't stretch if they are caught in rain. Here are my thoughts, but I want each of you to bring your own ideas."

The sun had long ago slipped below the horizon before their planning was completed. There had been intense discussions, but now most of the issues were settled. The most heated conversation was regarding Anan's idea of last resort. The most ardent disagreement came from Terja.

"You can't even consider this. The possibility of failure is too great."

"It might be the only thing that saves us, too," Anan said.

Terja folded his arms and met Anan in a contest of wills that lasted long past whcn most people would have relented. Finally he sighed and shook his head. "Only in a last attempt."

Anan nodded in agreement. "Only as a last resort."

CHAPTER FIFTEEN

ANAN LAY hidden in the dense brush and watched the Varas camp. The plans had been made and everyone was in their place. He hoped it would work. He'd used the corcra he and Terja made to create a giant web that would cover most of the slavers' camp. Hopefully the Varas would react to it as Morea had and fall into a gentle sleep.

"The moons are close."

Anan glanced at Terja and whispered in response. "The weaving is made. All I need to do is trigger the web, and the matama will cover everything like the pollen of a featherleaf tree in spring. But we don't know what effect it will have on the Varas. It may not work."

"Then we'll fight and free the captives without the darkness or the corcra."

He snaked his fingers along the back of Terja's neck and pulled him in for a kiss. Both relaxed into the embrace, and their lips pressed tight against each other.

"Twined Ones! Can't it wait until after we win?"

Anan glanced back to Morea with a faint smile. "It can, because we will. Just remember, your task is to take care of the captives. I don't want the Varas killing helpless people."

"Yes, Anan. You've told me at least a fingercount of times already. Stay out of sight, Morea. We don't want you hurt, Morea. We need you with the captives, Morea."

Anan gripped her chin and asked quietly, "And?"

She sighed softly. "And if I'm in danger Joven and Soneri will be in more danger because they'll watch to make sure I'm all right."

"Good. Now move to your spot. The obsidian sun is about to happen."

"All right." The young woman crawled through the brush without a sound and soon disappeared.

Anan glanced up again to find the first moon cutting into the sun. The twining moon came from the opposite direction and cut a similar sliver.

"You know, we could be the twin moons."

He glanced at Terja, his brows knitted together. "What're you talking about?"

"The twin moons, the twining moons. It's like us. Opposites that attract each other."

Anan shook his head. "We're facing a battle, and my twining mate is filling my head with kits' stories from Iceweaver's season."

Terja smirked and disappeared to his assigned spot without another word. But the tenderness coming through their connection left no doubt as to his feelings for Anan. He focused on their plan. Midday turning to twilight signaled the beginning of the attack. With a deft twist, he released the elaborate spell, and its strands fell, covering most of the encampment. He waited a moment, but there was no way to tell if it had worked. He readied himself to expect the worst and moved toward the first of the sentries.

Racing from one bit of cover to another, he quickly located the man. The slaver staggered, obviously affected but still conscious. Anan steeled himself for what he must do. Rising quickly he rushed the Varas, war club in hand. The guard only managed a startled grunt before the black warrior glass was imbedded in his chest. Anan slapped a hand over his mouth and rammed his knife into the side of his neck.

He held the struggling guard, keeping him silent for the heartbeat or two it took for his life to slip away.

Anan moved on to the next two slavers with equal success. But his part was freeing the captives. Terja and he were the only ones with enough power to open the iron of the chains.

After he silenced the last of his assigned guards, he ran to the captives, hoping everyone else had done as well. He slowed as the first of the Talac came into sight. Scanning the area, he could not find Terja. Quickly he checked their connection and found it as strong as ever. He slid to his knees beside one of the terrified Talac and motioned them to silence. He pulled matama from their connection in the hope this time he could unweave the iron, but the Ubica smiths foiled him again.

He felt someone approaching and spun, club in hand. Terja jumped backward, barely avoiding his swing. The look of terror on Terja's face told him how close he'd come to killing his twining. His stomach heaved at the thought. But he fought it down and motioned Terja close.

"I still can't unweave the iron. Let's see if we can unlock them together again."

"I felt your pull, that's how I found you."

Anan studied the lock and felt the energy feed into him from Terja. After several passes to find the locking sequence, he dropped his sight. "I can't find the thread again. What did we do differently before?"

"I'm not sure. I wasn't in condition to follow a complex weaving."

"Ravelings! What's different?"

Anan plunged back into his weaving, and this time Terja followed. He could see nothing but the threads of the dark gray mechanism. As he leaned closer, Terja laid his hand on Anan's shoulder.

Suddenly the threads of the locks were obvious. "That's it!"

Startled, Terja jumped away, losing contact.

"No, come here. When you touched me the lock revealed itself."

When they touched again, Anan could follow each of the steps. He breathed a sigh of relief when the iron matama slipped free and the lock clicked open.

"You did it," Terja whispered.

Anan smiled, but now that he knew the combination, it was like a boulder rolling down a hillside. Once started, it couldn't be stopped. He guided it from link to link and ring to ring, and in less time than they would have thought possible, the captives were free.

As the last shackle dropped to the ground, he turned to Terja with a triumphant smile. "They're all free. Let's get them out of here."

Terja stood and then jerked awkwardly, and a blinding pain shot through Anan's chest. Barely able to breathe, he looked up to see a crossbow quarrel sticking from Terja's chest. He caught Terja and lowered him to the ground as he fought the far too familiar pain of his twining being injured.

He looked behind Terja to find the one Soneri had called Kotu reloading a crossbow. Before Anan could move, the quarrel pointed at him.

"You're going to die, Talac. But you've destroyed everything. It won't be an easy death. I couldn't deal with both of you, so I killed the furless perversion."

Anan froze in place, more concerned about Terja. He probed their connection. *Not dead. Badly wounded. But not dead.* But soon it wouldn't matter. His mind scrambled for an answer. He heard the twang of a bowstring, and then the barbed bolt ripped into his gut. He grabbed the wooden shaft an instant before his body twisted with pain.

"That's how I like my victims. Scream for me."

Anan couldn't do more than watch as Kotu covered the distance between them. He fought his pain as the man stopped in front of him.

"Brave Talac. Let see how brave you are." Kotu reached down and twisted the blood-drenched shaft. Anan wavered on the edge of consciousness as the pain unfolded to new levels. His horror grew when he realized Kotu was opening his pants. He licked his lips as he pulled out his hard cock. "I will have pleasure from you before you die." He grabbed Anan's head, holding him so he was unable to move. Anan prepared for the final fight of his life.

The Varas suddenly lurched backward, clawing at his neck. Anan watched in abstract fascination as Kotu fought a cord tightening around his throat. Time stood still as the Varas's struggles slowed and finally stopped. With a final convulsion, Anan realized one source of evil was gone.

At that moment the first shaft of sunlight appeared and hit the yellow-white velvet of the person standing before him. Soneri.

"Where?"

Soneri knelt before him, and Anan gasped as his pain rebounded. A moment later he felt the cauterization spell some weavers used for healing.

"Morea and Joven are getting the captives out. The Varas are dead, except Geir and Xain. I can't find them. We need to go too. Can I move you?"

Every touch filled Anan with enough pain that he felt the need to vomit. He and Terja both needed to be healed. But he needed Terja to heal himself. He looked over to see bloody bubbles coming from Terja's lips.

"Heal him. Quickly. Then he and I can heal my wounds. It'll take both of us."

Soneri nodded and knelt beside Terja without argument. He snapped off the barbed quarrel head and then ripped out the shaft. Anan was too exhausted to follow Soneri's healing, but he hoped the big man was talented. He sank into himself, relieved to find their connection was not only in place but growing stronger.

"What? What happened?"

Terja. At least he would live.

"You were shot. Kotu. He's dead. I killed him. You need to help save Anan now." Soneri's eyes rolled until only the whites showed, and he collapsed.

Terja sat up, grimacing at the pain, and touched his fingers to Soneri's neck. After a moment he let out the breath he'd been holding. "He's all right."

Anan nodded, his hands wrapped tight against his stomach. "He healed you faster than he should have. Pulled the energy from himself."

He realized Terja wasn't listening. His eyes were fixed on Anan. He looked down and saw dark red blood drenched his lower body.

"Twined Ones, you're dying!"

TERJA CRAWLED as quickly as he could, ignoring the searing pain in his chest, and took Anan in his arms. Even without trying he could see Anan's life force unraveling. He knew if he didn't do something fast, his twined pairing would be no more.

"Heal yourself! Do it! I know you can. You healed me through akhir."

Anan shook his head. "Not enough left. I can't. Myself."

"No. No!"

Terja ripped matama from both their kilts, all he could reach surrounding them, and rammed them through their mating strand to Anan. The flood of energies forced itself through Anan's system. His body responded first by rejoining the worst of the bleeding veins. The blood loss slowed, and the repairing moved to the torn bowels.

The healing slowed before coming to a stop. Terja waited for a few moments and realized what had happened. "The healing matama are gone. I'm going to try spinning the injuries like I did before."

Anan stared at him, his breathing coming in gasps. "You are too injured. You could harm yourself, and we don't have the matama or a weaver to heal you."

"I don't give a strand! I'm healing you."

Anan mumbled, "Stubborn spinner."

Terja gritted his teeth and began without another word. First he yanked out the shaft. Anan moaned around clenched teeth as he quickly closed the worst of the injuries.

Terja focused on the repairs. Instinctively knowing where to work first, he matched up the severed organs and spun them together. He worked without keeping track of time but moving as quickly as he could. But by the time he closed the belly wound, the moons had moved until they were almost off the sun's face. He sent a silent plea to the Twined Ones.

"Anan? Talk to me. Twining, how are you?"

Anan's body arched like a bow as his moan filled the air. Terja hoped Soneri was right and the Varas were dead. He put his hands on Anan's chest as he panted, his velvet drenched with sweat.

"Anan. I think you're healed."

Anan gasped for a few moments before relaxing on the ground beside Terja. He waited patiently as Anan checked himself. At this point neither of them should be alive, so he wasn't going to question a little time. When Anan returned to him, there was a smile tugging at the corners of his mouth.

"Remind me that I never want to go anywhere without you. You did some amazing healing."

Terja sank onto the ground, finally allowing himself to relax. "I wasn't sure.... There wasn't really healing involved, just repairs."

"Repairs worked fine. I don't know if something might go wrong, but right now it looks good. I couldn't have done much better even if I'd had the healing matamas. I'm not sure that what you did on the inside wounds wasn't better."

Terja's chest filled with pride, but then he returned to their reality. "We need to leave. Now. We're going to have to drag Soneri out. But I don't know where Geir and Xain are. I don't want to be here."

They stood with each other's help, resettled their weapons, and each grabbed one of Soneri's arms. They'd pulled him a fingercount of paces before they had to stop for rest.

"This is going to take a while," said Terja.

"Not really."

The pair spun to find Geir with a crossbow trained on them. "I am not foolish Kotu. These tips are coated with daggerhorn poison, and you don't have enough of your Talac magic in all your precious weavings to heal its effect. So do as I say, or someone will die."

Anan let out a held breath. "You can only kill one of us. You can't reload before the other one gets to you. Let us take the captives and go to the grazing lands. You can worship your Red Gods and live out your life."

Geir clenched his teeth. "You will not rob me of my prize or my healer. I'll kill you all and take your pelts if that's what it takes. I know members of the House of the Sun will pay well for them. I'll have you all."

Soneri groaned, and Geir's gaze turned to the big man. "He is useless as a slave and worth a lot as bed covering." He pointed the crossbow at Soneri and gave a feral grin. "I think he should go first."

Terja strained to find him, but he was hidden to akhir. Somehow Xain had warded him. He hadn't even known that was possible. He could see Geir's muscles tense just before Anan's hand flashed out and a sliver of darkness buried itself in Geir's arm. He yanked upward, firing the bolt into the tree canopy.

Fueled on adrenaline, they rushed Geir and hit something as solid as an ironwood tree. Xain stepped from hiding, his hands dancing through a complex weaving. Terja could sense Anan trying to undo Xain's weaving, but it had been set long before, waiting to be tripped. The barrier seemed impregnable.

"Damn you to the Red Gods. My shield didn't hold against your thrice-damned warrior rock. But I have another way to bring you under control," Xain said.

His barrier rippled, and to their horror they saw Morea standing beside Geir and Xain, swaying slightly. His smile reached new levels of evil.

"You see, I do have a bargaining chit," Xain said. "And the slaves; they will not travel far since I've hamstrung them. Most of them will never walk again, none of them to the Kuri grazing lands."

"Release the girl and the Talac captives. These three will vouch for your safe passage. I will go with you," Terja said.

Xain's eye's narrowed, and his tongue ran along his lips. "You would surrender yourself, spinner?" His eye's darted over Terja's bare skin as his look calculated the intent.

"So I swear by the First Twining."

"I will enjoy you, Talac," Xain said.

"But everyone is released. I'm worth more than a crowd of broken, furry weavers."

Xain narrowed his eyes again as he considered the proposal, and Geir stepped forward, his wounded arm at his side.

The ground rolled under their feet, throwing everyone off balance. Terja realized the careful webbing of captivity was in ruins from the attack. He recognized Joven's unique flavor, surprised at the young man's skill. As they regained their feet, Joven dashed from hiding to grab Morea and pull her from harm's way.

Xain burned away the barrier as he had each of the clan weavings while Anan waited intently, his bow held in ready. Terja was equally prepared with shield and staff in place. He yelled to Joven. "Take Morea and care for the captives. Lead them back to the Kuri lands."

At that moment he lunged forward to try to catch Geir unaware. But Geir was a seasoned veteran and easily blocked his attack. Terja moved into one of the staff patterns he had learned and focused on Geir and his blade. He jumped back to avoid the sword's sweep. As they stalked each other, he caught a glimpse of Anan closing with Xain.

ANAN NOCKED an arrow, certain it was a wasted effort to shoot one before the barrier was gone. But at the same time he pushed a trickle of weaving toward the ground where Xain stood. He hoped to create a trip spell from the plants surrounding Xain's feet. He wove carefully, in tiny movements, until Xain was tethered to the ground.

Anan heard the clang of metal against wood as Terja and Geir clashed. The attacks were increasingly fierce, which concerned Anan, knowing that Terja was still weak, having been healed only moments ago. Anan glanced toward them and found Terja being forced into a retreat by Geir's flurry of attacks.

Xain moved and drew Anan back into their battle. He tried to slide his foot, then glared at Anan. After releasing his feet with a twist of his hand, Xain made a series of slashes at Anan with his long knife, which Anan danced backward to avoid. Anan tossed his bow aside and ripped his war club from his sash.

Xain spun his knife back so it ran along the underside of his arm. With one arm effectively converted into a blade, he moved upon Anan in a battle frenzy. The ironwood of the club stopped the blade as effectively as anything crafted from metal. With a twist, Anan trapped Xain's blade in the serrated teeth formed by the obsidian shards of the club. He pushed the weapon backward, the tip slicing into Xain's arm as he flung himself back to avoid the deadly warrior glass.

TERJA STEPPED backward under the hail of strikes from Geir. His newly healed wounds left him weakened, and Geir's experience began to show even through his own injury.

Driven back farther by a sudden flurry of attacks, Geir grabbed the loaded crossbow and swung it toward him. Terja grabbed his shield and threw it toward Geir. The disc flicked forward with more speed than Terja would have thought possible, slicing through the crossbow, cutting the bowstring and rendering it useless.

Geir's face contorted as he screamed and swung his short sword toward Terja.

Terja grabbed his staff and stood ready but saw his shield bank and spin toward them. As Geir stepped forward, Terja's shield slammed into the back of his neck and a scream erupted from Geir. At that moment, Terja jumped forward and drove the toothed staff into his throat.

Geir crumbled, a look of disbelief etched across his face.

GEIR'S SCREAM penetrated Anan's battle haze, and he smiled as the cry came to an abrupt halt. Terja had succeeded. An instant later an enraged Xain flew toward him in a flurry of strikes. He bellowed his return attack and hammered Xain, forcing the traitor to retreat along the path they had just traveled. He saw they were nearing the spot where he'd woven the plants to try to trip the traitor. Xain wavered when he stepped on the rough ground, and Anan pressed his attack.

Anan's last swing sent Xain stumbling. He dodged another of Anan's vicious attacks and jumped backward. The traitor sprinted a short distance before activating another weaving hidden in the landscape.

Anan saw his bow and dove for it. He nocked, drew, and released his arrow in one fluid motion as the weave around Xain rippled. Anan quickly sent another arrow after the first and then tried to break the warp of Xain's spell. But his target had vanished. Anan studied the surroundings closely, thinking Xain used some type of camouflage weaving. He detected a ripple, like a transparent cloth fluttering to the ground, but then the spell disappeared.

"I hope the longtooth feed on your carcass!" Anan bellowed.

He glanced at Terja as he walked beside him. "I think he did a weaving of unseeing. My teacher explained them to me. Some people say it takes you to the Great Weaving to be born again. But Alo thought it created a rip in the weavings between existences, and a weaver could hide in it. But I don't know for certain. I couldn't break it, and I'm not interested in trying to follow him."

"Don't we need to hunt him down?" Terja asked.

"No, he's a runaway slave to the Varas, and they feed runaways to the river serpent. Soon all the Talac will know about him and might give him to the deathspinners. Either way, I don't think he's a danger to us right now. Later…." Anan shrugged.

XAIN PRESSED himself against the trunk of an ironwood tree and shoved the obsidian tipped arrow through his side until the barbed head ripped through the skin of his back. A soft gasp of pain escaped his lips, but he'd suffered much worse and survived. He braced himself again and grunted through clenched teeth as he snapped off the sharp head. The pain ripping through his body was simply the latest wave of agony Xain found himself submerged under. He didn't dare use any of the matama his kilt still contained. He might need those on his trip back to the river and the Burning Twins.

He pushed himself to his feet and stumbled forward, a hand pressed hard against the seeping wound. One foot trailed the other as he ducked into the brush, wanting to make certain none of the Talac found him. He was well aware of the consequences. He worked his way slowly up a steep hill, stopping for rest several times as his kilt became soaked with his own blood.

He reached the ridge to discover how close they had been to reaching the Varas lands, and success. As he started down the steep hillside, he glanced over his shoulder and shot a poisonous glare to the west.

CHAPTER SIXTEEN

ANAN LAID his hands on either side of the youngster's leg and wove the tendons together. "Hold still. The closer I can align everything, the better you will be able to walk when it heals."

This was one of the most severely injured Talac, and he had almost died from Xain's work. But all the captives were in worse condition than he and Terja had hoped. Their own wounds, while largely healed, made them both tire easily. But they were thankful to be alive.

"There," Anan told the young man, "no foot races for you, though. You're still going to need help getting around for another moon or so."

"Thank you, Anan. It already feels better." He wiped tears from his eyes. "Thank you for saving us. I didn't think I would ever see the grasslands again. Then yesterday—"

"You'll be fine. Just give the Twined Ones time to help you heal."

Soneri gathered the injured man in his arms and carried him to a shaded area so he could rest. The big man had recovered quickly from overextending himself healing Terja although Anan had a suspicion that he and Terja dragging him to camp had left more cuts and bruises.

Terja walked beside him and rubbed his hand over Anan's shoulder. "You should be celebrating. We won."

Anan's lips quirked into a smile. "I could say the same for you. I'll feel something once I have time." He turned to stare into Terja's eyes. "They think I'm someone wonderful. I just did what I had to do, and I had four of you helping. We couldn't even save everyone. Some of them died before we could heal them."

Terja wrapped his fingers over Anan's shoulder and squeezed. "The others feel the guilt too, even Morea. We saved almost everyone. Joven and Soneri are readying the bodies for the unraveling."

Two of the former captives moved past, one helping the other walk. Terja shook his head. "The scars we can't see worry me too. For some the trauma will never leave."

Morea stopped them. "Here. Eat. You can't keep going until you fall over from exhaustion and lack of food." She handed them each a bowl of soup.

Anan cupped the warm meal between his hands and took a sip. "That's delicious, Morea. Where did you find the ingredients?" A terrible thought flashed through his mind. "You didn't use any of the Varas food, did you? Xain might have poisoned it."

Morea rolled her eyes. "By the Twined Ones, Anan. Do you think I'm stupid? The meat is springtail. Joven brought it down with a sling. He's good with the weapon. Soneri found the rest. His family traveled a lot and harvested whatever was in season as they did. He knows which plants are good to eat. Just to be sure, I did a weaving to check that nothing bad was on them." She scowled. "Now start eating and stop talking."

Anan watched as she left, a slight smile on his lips. He was still concerned for the girl, but she seemed to be handling the changing situation. Terja sighed as he finished the last of the meal.

"I know. I'm exhausted too. I'd like to curl up under a nice wide guardian bush and sleep until the spring ice melt."

Terja looked at his kilt and then Anan's. "We've used up almost all the matama and the silk I'd unwound. Fortunately we didn't need to use your crazed idea against anyone. But I need to gather more matama, and most of what is around this camp is sickness matama, which isn't good for anything."

"What about against someone?"

Terja hesitated, then shrugged. "I don't know. I can spin some and make sure it's sealed away from everything else. We've done so many things I've never heard of before that I just don't know."

"Good idea, keeping it safe from affecting anyone."

Soneri carried a patient to the bedding and laid her down gently. Anan saw she still had the slave collar and wrist irons.

"Terja, I need some help to get her irons off."

Terja laid his hands on Anan's shoulders, which strengthened their connection. Anan pulled energy, and began to look for the lock thread as he had before. By this time the method was familiar. But as he began to trace the lock, he felt Terja following some of the sickness matama. As they worked together, Terja tugged on the threads suddenly, and Anan fell backward with a yelp.

"What in the Paired Ones was that?" Anan asked.

"I pulled some sickness matama. I didn't think it would hurt."

"It ate through the iron, like some potent venom. It almost dropped onto her."

"Strands! I'm so sorry. I didn't know it would do that. Maybe we can use it for something. But I won't spin any more without warning you first."

They went back to work on the young woman, first removing the irons and then healing her wounds. By the time they'd finished, the sun touched the tops of the trees to the west. Anan stood, wavering in place. "Take her to one of the mats so she can rest, Soneri."

Anan watched the muscular man gently lift the woman and carry her to a bed for rest. He felt Terja's light touch.

"We're almost done."

"Did you check them? We don't need any more traps like Joven had."

"As much as I could. But there is a lot of damage to these people."

Terja wrapped his arms around Anan. "This is like nothing anyone else has suffered. The Talac captives were abused every way possible until even the undamaged ones don't have the strength for the trip back to the grasslands. Soneri had to carry most of them to us and then back to their bedding. We need to start the trip home. I have no idea how to do it with all these injured people."

"The uninjured can pull them."

170

The pair turned to find Soneri and Joven standing behind them. Anan shook his head. They *were* exhausted, to allow the pair to walk up on them undetected. Before he could respond, Terja asked the question for both of them. "How? They can't be carried over your shoulder across the savanna through the Iceweaver's season."

"No, but we can make the same drags we used to move our camps. It only takes two long poles tied together at one end and a carrying platform on the other. I could probably train the biggest of your kuri to pull them if we were on the plains."

Anan considered for a moment, but the idea seemed sound. "Take whoever is able to help you. I don't have a better idea. Xain is out there somewhere and may be creating more traps for one of us to stumble into."

Soneri spun, grabbed Joven by the arm, and disappeared around a tent. Terja turned to Anan. "I am concerned about Xain. I agree, he is out there somewhere. I'd like to believe your arrow sent him to the Burning Twins, but I can't relax until we are at the Kuri winter encampment. I have a few of the captives who are alert but still unable to walk on the guard for any strange weaving. Xain learned things in the pits of the Varas no Talac should ever know, and now he uses them against his own people."

Anan shook his head. "Xain has no people. He is a mad longtooth with no pack. The Varas allowed him to live only because of what he was willing to do. Now any Talac will happily cut his throat."

"Come on. We have a few other people to treat, and I need your help."

Anan moved toward a small group of Talac huddled under a featherleaf tree. He waited as the matama built along their connection. One of the victims cried out softly. Anan released his weaving over him and sent him into a deep sleep. Once he was unconscious, Anan used his knife to drain the infection from several wounds. "These people will be scarred for the rest of their lives."

"Yes, but at least these marks will fade with time."

Anan looked across the forms huddled on the ground and felt a wash of resolve as he studied the broken people around him.

"They're all Kuri now. I think they will find more solace with people who understand what they've been through."

"I've heard some of them talking to each other," Anan said. "They don't want to return to their home clans, even if they could. For many of them there's no other choice. Their villages were wiped from the grasslands."

"Some of them won't live through the journey. Iceweaver doesn't tolerate the weak. It will take us several moons to get to the Kuri's winter village. It's on the opposite side of the grasslands."

"They survived the Varas. At least the Iceweaver is not hunting you down to kill you. She weaves her tapestry carefully."

The younger trio rejoined them. Anan glanced toward Soneri. "Did you find what you needed?"

"Yes, several of the people were happy to have something to do." Soneri gazed into the blue sky and began to speak without looking at any of them. "I heard what you were saying about Iceweaver. She may be merciless, but she doesn't cut the throat of the person who slept against you the night before to fight off a chill and then throw the body into the brush for the animals to quarrel over while the rest listen to the bones crunch and shake from fear of being next."

Morea put her hand on Soneri's arm. "You never showed any fear."

Soneri patted her arm gently. "There is a difference between bravery and no hope. I had no hope. When this—" He ran his hands down his torso. "—is worth more than my life to the House of the Sun. There is no hope."

Anan motioned them away. "I have a few more injured to treat. But we need to finalize our plans. The trip back must start soon. Every day we delay means fewer will survive the trip. We need clothing for the winter and weapons for hunting even if we aren't attacked. Hopefully we can find enough daggerhorn and springtail to hunt for meat and tanned skins before we are in the worst of Iceweaver's season."

"We have more than you think," Joven said. "Soneri and I scavenged the Varas camp. The extra tents can be cut into clothing.

But tents and poles were all we took. You'd already warned us the food might be poisoned. We'll just have to find a way."

The three younger Talac turned to leave Terja and Anan to their weaving. Before they had taken more than a few steps, Terja stopped them. "I'm sure he's well on his way to the Varas. But take this in case you need it."

Soneri stared at the toothed staff Terja offered and stood unmoving. Terja pressed it into his hands. "Take it. We got it from the slaver who had targeted Joven. But it's Talac. I checked to make certain it was not contaminated with Varas matama. It works well against the long knives of the Varas."

Soneri paused for a moment and then wrapped his fingers around the haft with an almost loving caress. "This was my father's. He had it when the Varas attacked. But he was hit by a fingercount of quarrels in the first wave. They would have killed me too but for the color of my velvet."

Joven stepped close and rubbed his hand along the back of Soneri's neck. "None of what happened is your fault. The Varas attacked us. Their perverted reasons don't make any of it our fault."

Soneri met Joven's gaze and draped an arm across his shoulders. "I know. But there are still difficult times coming."

Terja released the staff to Soneri's grip. "Take the staff, then. Joven told us they were the weapons of the spellspinners, but I do not need it, and it holds special meaning for you. Go make a final search through the Varas camp. Whatever is left, burn it."

"Yes, burn everything. I don't want a trace of the Varas left behind," Anan said.

Soneri gave them a grim smile. "We will take care of it, and be assured we will wipe out all traces."

ANAN AND Terja moved through the camp, checking on the last of the survivors. They made their way to the edge of the clearing. Both spun, weapons drawn at a slight rustling. But when they overlaid their sight over the ground, they saw a single glowing silver thread. Anan glanced at Terja.

"I've never seen a thread like that before."

Terja considered it for a moment before sucking a breath between his teeth. "We have seen it. This is the thread the Twined Ones surrounded us with."

A chill flowed through Anan as he realized Terja was right. Without another word, they began to follow the iridescent thread into the thickening trees. They reached an almost impassible thicket, and Terja came to a stop.

"This would be a perfect ambush. Are we walking to our deaths?"

Anan glanced his direction, then created a weaving and sent it along the web. He tested the thread every way he knew and found nothing more than a strengthening pull from the Twined Ones. The final test left him with the taste similar to the one he'd sensed moons ago when the gods first listened to their plea.

"It even tastes like the Twined Ones. If Xain is this good, then we won't last long."

Terja studied him for a moment, then nodded. "We need to move quickly. This all sets me on edge."

The pair plunged forward. Anan noticed the strand thickened as they followed. They reached the top of the ridge and found it encircled with trees more ancient than any Anan had seen before. When they entered the circle, he noticed the strand they had been following was unraveling into more threads than Anan could count, spreading in all directions. They studied it for a moment, and then Terja glanced at Anan.

"I think you should create the webbing like last time."

Anan nodded and began pulling matama as he wove walls around them. The threads of energy intertwined until a solid shape came into existence. And as it had at the beginning of their quest, other threads came in until the world outside their small enclosure was completely blocked. Anan's heart pounded. It was never good to attract the attention of the gods on some kind of regular basis. But the next sound sent chills through his body that threatened to paralyze him.

As months before, two of the largest deathspinners Anan could imagine worked their way to the lower branches and studied him and Terja. Anan's nerves thinned until they were ready to snap.

Give us time, younglings. We will change into an easier form in a moment.

Anan swallowed hard and glanced at Terja. The spinner was flushed, but his mouth was set firmly as he stared at the two deathspinners. As Anan turned back, the air around them rippled, and two familiar Talac stood before them.

"Better?" asked First Weaver.

Anan nodded but then swallowed hard enough that it seemed to echo through their small space. By now he realized they'd been summoned, but he wasn't certain why.

"Yes, that's... easier," said Terja.

First Spinner leaned in and kissed First Weaver softly on the cheek. "Love, they are no more comfortable with us than they were before. We should at least tell them they have done well."

"I think you just did." With a smile he turned to Anan and Terja. "You saved everyone who could be saved and some that we still don't know how you managed. You shouldn't lose any more, at least not to their time with the Varas. You used your gifts well, but you have discovered there are limits to your newly expanded abilities."

First Spinner took up the litany. "I'm sure you've realized by now, only half the task is done. You have the people to rebuild the Kuri. But now you must guide them across the savanna, through Iceweaver's season."

"We are also here to tell you that you are not released from your bloodweaving until you reach the Kuri homelands. But you have help now, and know that, failure or success, it will be with you combined as one."

Terja began, "Yes, First Weaver. We know we are not finished. And that Xain escaped." He glanced to Anan, who nodded his agreement and sent him a warm caress through their connection.

Before he could continue, First Spinner began to chuckle. "I see you have gotten some skill with the bond between you. Remember you will always know what the other feels, even if not the words. But do not assume you know what they are thinking."

"You are twined, even if all the Kuri ceremonies were not followed. Your bonding has been woven in the heat of battle. But that doesn't mean there is no possibility of severing it. Treat it as it should be treated, like a precious weaving of the ancestors."

Anan waited. While this was good to know, he wondered what else First Twining had in mind.

"Now for the last information we have. Although you have not finished your bloodweaving, you can petition us for help. It may or may not be within our powers, but when possible we will render you what assistance First Twining can."

Anan didn't know if he should feel relief or apprehension. He'd learned from a young age that pleas to the gods often didn't turn out well for the petitioner. But he nodded; the trip to the winter village of the Kuri would not be easy. The time might come when they were so desperate that they petitioned assistance from First Twining.

He nodded in their direction and pulled Terja close. "We hope we don't need help, but thank you for its offer."

First Weaver smiled at them. "Ah, a wise youngling. You're right. Everything has a cost. But know you can do so should times become so dire."

Anan waited for more revelations, but First Twining seemed finished. "Thank you. It's always good to have another plan. We will not abuse the help."

First Spinner chuckled and seemed to be about to grasp Anan's shoulder, when he remembered what he was. He shifted his gaze between the pair before turning back to First Weaver. "It's time. We've given the information."

The two shifted back to their animal form and scurried up the tree. The web around them began to fade when Anan heard the last words of First Weaver echo through him.

You love him. Keep him safe.

AFTER A fingercount of days to prepare, they were ready to begin the trek back to the clan's homelands. Soneri and Joven had built the drags, and the people who couldn't walk were loaded onto their platforms. Extra gear served as padding, and other sleds carried the rest of their supplies.

Anan shouted instructions and directed people toward the path. The first few Talac had started along the trail to the west as soon as the sun appeared on the eastern horizon. Their first day's travel would be a series of stops and starts as they worked out problems and allowed people to rest. Anan had given Soneri instructions on where to stop for the night, and it was a location they should be able to travel in a half day's journey.

Terja listened to the discussion around the camp and sent encouragement to Anan along their connection. He turned and smiled at Terja, then walked over to join him.

"The connection still seems to be getting stronger. I can find you easily now."

"I'd agree. It seems easier and easier to follow you."

Anan's brows twisted. "Today might not be the best day to do that. So many things could go wrong."

"Some will, but most won't. We've done what we could. Let's just get through the day."

"What about Xain? He may be back at some point."

"If he does, then we'll deal with it. Right now he has no one to help him. He won't be trying to trail us. Once he reaches the Varas, though, and tells them we have a sun-touched as well as a spinner…. Well, I don't know what will happen."

Terja considered the people walking past them in clumps of two or three, almost all of them pulling one of Soneri's sleds. He would be glad to begin putting more distance between them and the Varas. There was much to be done and a chill in the wind. He knew not all of them would survive this trip. They'd done what they could, but the ferocity of Iceweaver was well known.

An enormous hawk screamed above them, and with a few lazy flaps of its wings, it quickly became a dot on the western horizon. He glanced at Anan to find him with his gaze locked on the disappearing bird.

"What?" asked Terja.

"That was a red-winged diver. They are huge, so big they hunt daggerhorns. They never come this far east."

"So it was lost. It doesn't mean anything."

"That bird was Silbre's totem. That's the first one I've seen since the attack on the Kuri."

Terja started to argue, but a warm breeze filled with the scents of the grasslands in high summer blew across his face, and he nodded.

"We could use all the guidance we can find."